BY
LAW AND
LOVE

When God builds a new society

By

David Harley

Table of Contents

Dedication

To my darling wife, Rosemary,

partner in life and in mission,

who wishes she had this book when, as a new graduate,

she was asked to lead a group study on Leviticus

Acknowledgement

I am so grateful to Paul and Ping Lee, my Singaporean church friends, for their support and encouragement in the writing of my two earlier titles and this new book. I am especially indebted to Ping for her editorial skill. Although she will want to kill me for writing this, or even mentioning her name, I think she is the most amazing editor one could wish for, and I am greatly indebted to her.

I also would like to thank my dear wife, Rosemary for her love and patience, when house chores were left undone and she still encouraged me to finish the book.

Many thanks too to Petra Abbott, a member of our local church, Holy Trinity Church Exeter, who read the book from cover to cover, made insightful comments and asked pertinent questions that resulted in making the book more reader friendly.

I have always appreciated the work of Langham Preaching and have been involved in some of their preaching seminars in Asia. It was extremely kind of Jonathan Lamb, former director of Langham Preaching and now minister at large with Keswick Ministries, to take time to read the book and to recommend it in his foreword.

I am glad to publish this new book through Amazon and am grateful to Matthew and his editorial team at Amazon for their guidance and efficiency.

About the Author

DAVID HARLEY studied at Cambridge University and then Bristol University, and holds doctorates from Columbia International University in the USA and Utrecht University in the Netherlands. He and his wife, Rosemary, have worked together in ministry and theological education for more than fifty years.

After serving in an Anglican church in London, they served as missionaries in Ethiopia for five years, before joining the faculty of All Nations Christian College, in the UK. After they had worked there for eight years, David was appointed Principal. He subsequently served in Singapore as Dean of Discipleship Training Centre and lecturer at Trinity Theological College, before becoming General Director of OMF International. Now retired, he continues an international ministry in churches, conferences and theological colleges.

David has written five books, including *By Faith and Failure,* which examines the life of Abraham, and *By Word and Wonders,* which looks at the character of God as revealed in the book of Exodus. Both of these titles are being published through Amazon.

David and Rosemary have three children and five grandchildren.

Foreword

'All scripture is useful' wrote Paul, in his great declaration about the power and relevance of the Bible. But I suspect many of us have raised an eyebrow when it comes to Leviticus, Numbers, and Deuteronomy. Is it really profitable to wade through long lists of ancient laws, ceremonial practices, wilderness meanderings, and threats of judgment?

And even if we admit to the importance of the whole Bible, the preacher then faces another question. How do I make sense of these passages and present their truth with relevance to a twenty-first-century congregation? Many of us steer clear of such Bible books.

But I can predict that as you read the pages which follow, you will have the same experience that I had. I kept thinking - the apostle Paul was right! These neglected Bible books really are useful for teaching, training, and equipping God's people. And there are several reasons for this illuminating experience.

First, David Harley has had many years of experience in explaining the Bible in different cultural contexts. He understands both the culture of the Bible and the culture of our contemporary churches and societies, and he knows how to make the connections.

Second, he has grasped the essential meaning of each section of the Bible books he tackles and expresses this with extraordinary simplicity and clarity such that we immediately see their significance and purpose. These pages provide a great example of how to explain demanding sections of the Bible in the light of the New Testament, especially the work of the Lord Jesus.

Third, we immediately see the connection between our lives and our world. It's like reading from today's newspaper, with references to the global pandemic, the refugee crisis, sexual health, the environment, human flourishing, justice and equality, and social reform. And it speaks to personal challenges, too, whether coping with failure, handling criticism or disappointment, confronting sin and temptation, or tackling division in the church. We begin to understand the powerful relevance of these Bible passages to the people of God in every age, our own included, and we find a lovely combination of accessible explanations of difficult passages, along with wise, practical application to today's world and everyday life.

In addition, each chapter is crafted in ways that enable a preacher or home group leader, or youth worker to explain some of these core passages in ways that are clear and relevant. With discussion questions added, this is a wonderful handbook for explaining little-read Bible books to others.

But I found that the most significant thing that impacted me as I finished each section was the overwhelming sense of God's goodness and faithfulness. How extraordinary that he cares so much about the day-to-day life of his people, about our sin and failure, and our redemption and flourishing.

I am sure you will benefit from these pages as much as I have and will share my hope that David doesn't put his pen down but continues to help us see the powerful relevance of the scriptures for today's world.

Jonathan Lamb

Minister-at-large, Keswick Ministries, and former Director, Langham Preaching

Preface

When we were living in Singapore, Paul and Choy Ping Lee expressed appreciation for a series of sermons I had given on Abraham and encouraged me to publish them in a book. They offered both to edit and publish the book through their newly formed publication company, Zoie. I was the General Director of OMF International at the time and with too many responsibilities to work on the book, but subsequent to my retirement, we published *By Faith and Failure* on the life of Abraham in 2007. Three years later, we produced a second book, *By Word and Wonders,* which looks at the dramatic story of the Exodus in which God rescues slaves and adopts them as his people. Both books were subsequently reprinted, with added questions for groups and individual reflection, and translated into a number of Asian languages.

While on the staff faculty at All Nations Christian College, in the UK, I lectured on the first five books of the Bible, which included Leviticus, Numbers and Deuteronomy. These books are less widely read or appreciated, yet they contain great truths about God and practical lessons about how we can live as his people. Leviticus helps us understand the holiness of God and the reason why Jesus died. Numbers records both the dramatic struggle of immigrants on their journey to freedom and the problems of spiritual leadership faced by Moses. Deuteronomy reminds us how much God loves people and wishes them to love him in return.

Once again encouraged by our friends in Singapore, and being heavily dependent on their editorial comment and advice, I wrote this third volume, *By Law and Love,* which seeks to unpack the central message of these three books, go beyond the details of the laws and ancient rituals they contain, and examine what God is saying to us through these books today.

These three books, Leviticus, Numbers and Deuteronomy, were very highly regarded by the Old Testament people of God, by the first disciples and by the Lord Jesus himself. I pray that this book will help you to see why they were so important to them, and what spiritual truths God wishes us to learn from them.

David Harley

Exeter, UK

2022

Introduction

We were about to begin the evening service when Claire, a keen member of our church, turned to me and said: "David, please help. I am trying to read the Bible in a year but I am really struggling with Leviticus and its endless laws. If I read another law, I shall burst into tears!" I sympathised with her and suggested that there were other ways of familiarising herself with the whole Bible than reading it from beginning to end. She was grateful when I offered to send her some notes on the early chapters of Leviticus. That exchange inspired me to turn my notes on Leviticus, Numbers and Deuteronomy into a book.

Many Christians today struggle with a book like Leviticus and are not quite sure what they are meant to get out of it. To be honest, they struggle with many parts of the Old Testament. They wonder how the Old Testament can be relevant today. It is so ancient. Well, it is called *Old* Testament, isn't it? Some of it is really hard to understand. Take: "I am become like a bottle in the smoke" (Psalm 119:83). What on earth does that mean? Or "Feed me with apples for I am sick with love" (Song of Solomon 2:5). When you are in love, what is the use of apples? The Old Testament was written thousands of years ago and is all about camels, wells, chariots and living in the desert. Most of it was written long before the coming of Jesus. He is the light of the world, so why spend time in the dark, some may wonder?

If we find much of the Old Testament difficult to understand, it is no surprise that there are some books we tend to ignore altogether. I recently heard of a survey conducted among Christian students at university asking which books of the Old Testament they found most helpful and which they did not like. The responses showed that they enjoyed books containing narrative, telling the stories of characters

3

like Abraham, Moses, David and Ruth. They appreciated some of the Psalms but not others, and they were inspired by a few passages in the Prophets like Isaiah 53. The books they did not like at all were Leviticus, Numbers and Deuteronomy.

So, one might ask, why bother to study these three books? That is a question you may have asked yourself. Many Christians skip over these books and in many churches few sermon series are preached from them. Yet, they comprise a major part of the first five books of the Bible, which form the foundation of all subsequent biblical teaching. These three books were regarded by Jesus and the first Christians as being inspired by God and authoritative in their teaching. Jesus quoted from each of them and he referred to Deuteronomy more than to any other book in the Bible. Both before and after his resurrection, Jesus taught the disciples that all the Scriptures, which included Leviticus, Numbers and Deuteronomy, pointed towards his coming and would be fulfilled. The apostle Paul added that the Scriptures were written to help us understand the great plan of God, to help us grow spiritually, and to warn us not to emulate the mistakes that God's people made in the past.

What can we learn from Leviticus, Numbers and Deuteronomy? One helpful way to approach them is to consider the books as God's guide to living as his people. At the beginning of Leviticus, the people of God were still spiritual babies, like recent converts. They had been rescued from the terrible conditions in which they were living as slaves to the king of Egypt. They were despised by the dominant community, oppressed and abused, with little hope that things would ever change. Many of them had given up believing in the God their ancestors worshipped and had turned instead to worship the gods of the Egyptians (Joshua 24:14). But some hung on to their belief in the God of Abraham and they cried out to him for help. In response to that cry, God sent Moses to deliver them. He took them out of the land of slavery, led them across the Red Sea and through the wilderness to

Mount Sinai. There he formally adopted them as his people and taught them how they should live.

At that point the people of Israel had been dramatically rescued from slavery and freed from years of oppression at the hands of the Egyptians. They had witnessed miraculous displays of God's power and an awesome demonstration of his glory on Mount Sinai. They praised God after crossing the Red Sea, and they began to believe in the god of their ancestors. But they were young in their faith. Everything was so new. They understood so little of how they were to live as the people of God.

They needed a basic course of instruction at this early stage of their life of faith. They had to learn how to pray and worship God, and they needed people who could guide and instruct them in their spiritual development. They had to learn that God was concerned with every area of their lives, and that, in everything they did, he wished them to adhere to standards that were for their benefit and would reflect his character. That was the function of the laws and instructions we find in the book of **Leviticus**. It was a manual for godly or holy living for people who had recently come to saving faith. Although the world the people of Israel lived in was very different from ours and many of the instructions, they were given seem totally foreign, even repulsive, to our modern way of thinking, the principles underlying the teachings in Leviticus contain eternal truth that is just as relevant for us today.

After their epic rescue the people of Israel could not stay on the mountain forever. They had to press on towards the land that God had promised to give them, where they could become an independent nation worshipping and serving the God who had saved them. So, they set out on their journey through the wilderness and the book of **Numbers** is a record of that great adventure. It is not a story of a triumphant spiritual walk with God, but it is a story of life as it really is. It demonstrates that the life of faith is not an easy path to tread and there are many hard lessons that will be learned along the way.

Almost as soon as they had left the shelter of Mount Sinai, the people of God encountered problems and revealed the true nature of their hearts. Rather than being grateful for all that God had done, they became very grumpy and behaved like spoiled children. Instead of marching straight into the land God said he would give them, they spent years going round in circles and ended up falling into serious sexual temptation.

Fortunately, the journey through the wilderness did not last forever and eventually the people of Israel returned to the edge of the Promised Land. By this time Moses was 120 and nearing the end of his life. The whole generation of Hebrews who had been saved from Egypt had passed on and it was a new younger generation who were going to enter the land. In a series of impassioned sermons Moses reminded them of what God had done and taught them again the fundamental truths of their faith. He sought to explain how they were to apply the word of God to the new challenges they would face and their new lifestyle in the Promised Land. He challenged them to remember all that God had done for them. He warned them of the dangers of materialism and self-reliance, and he set down the laws of God in a more systematic and comprehensive way. The book of **Deuteronomy**, which contains those sermons, is not in essence a book about the law, even though it has the misleading title "the second law." It is about love, God's love for his people and the love he longs to receive from them. God wishes his people to live in a way which reflects his character and his holiness, in a relationship built not on a set of laws but on love.

Section 1

House Rules

How Do We Live with God?

Chapter 1

A Life of Prayer

Many Christians find it difficult to approach God in prayer. We are not sure when to pray or what to pray about. Sometimes we pray because we are afraid or worried. Sometimes we pray when things have worked out well and we want to thank God for what has happened. At other times we realize we have done something wrong or said something unkind and hurt someone. We want to say sorry to God and to ask him to help us to be better people. Even though prayer may be difficult for us we also find ourselves wanting to pray for our families and friends. Occasionally we may pray for our local church, community, nation and the wider world.

After God led his people out of Egypt, he began to teach them how they could pray to and worship him. The rituals he gave them seem strange to our modern ears, but as we try to understand their significance, we will gain a deeper understanding of prayer and worship and realise more clearly how it is possible for sinful people like us to approach a holy God with confidence and enjoy close fellowship with him.

Leviticus 1–7

The people of Israel have been saved from slavery and adopted as God's children. Once they have completed the building of the Tabernacle, the glory of God descends from the mountain and enters the Holy of holies in the Tabernacle. God is now living among his people. That is an incredible privilege. It is also rather scary. After all, it is one thing to have a priest or a nun living next to you. It is something else to have the creator of the universe as your next-door neighbour.

God calls the Israelites a holy people. Yet the people know they are far from perfect. Many times, they failed to live by God's standards. So, what will happen if, even unintentionally, they do something which displeases God? How can they be forgiven? How can their status as a holy people be restored? How can they live close to God and maintain their relationship with him? What should they do if they want God to help them or their family, as he is the one who has promised to supply all their needs? How do they thank God for hearing and answering their prayers?

These are the kind of questions that the book of Leviticus seeks to answer. The book is given its name because much of it deals with the duties of the Levites, who belong to the tribe of Levi. They are responsible for the maintenance of the Tabernacle and the rituals of sacrifice. But the book is concerned with much more than the religious duties of these priests. It painstakingly instructs the people on how they are to draw near to God in worship and how they are to live with him.

Leviticus is one of the most difficult books to read in the Bible. Many Christians find it perplexing, even repulsive in parts, and cannot understand the strange and rather bloody ceremonies it describes. However, if we can get beyond our natural reluctance to look seriously at this book, we shall discover it has much to teach us. Leviticus shows us how we can love God, serve him, experience his healing and his blessing, and live in a way that pleases him. It spells out how we should love and care for others, and contains one of the most important commands in the whole Bible: "You shall love your neighbour as yourself" (Leviticus 19:18).

The book also helps us to understand the significance of the death of Jesus. It reveals how a holy God loves us so much that he has made it possible for us to be forgiven and to live in fellowship with him. The New Testament constantly refers back to Leviticus to explain the meaning of the cross. The letter to the Hebrews especially helps us grasp what Jesus has done for us as our High Priest and our perfect sacrifice.

The worship that is detailed in Leviticus centres on sacrifice and ritual offerings. This pattern of worship is typical of the cultures of the Ancient Near East, and is a way of worship that the Israelites can understand and find meaningful. Through it they can express penitence and gratitude, and enjoy fellowship with the God who has blessed them in so many ways.

Five different sacrifices are described in the opening chapters of Leviticus. Each type of sacrifice differs as to what is offered, why it is offered, how it is offered, how much of it is eaten and who is allowed to eat it. Each focuses on different aspects of worship, such as confession, forgiveness, thanksgiving, intercession, cleansing and restoration.

SEEKING FORGIVENESS (1:1-17)

The sacrifice which is offered most frequently is the **burnt offering** (Leviticus 1:1–17). The offering may be a bull, a sheep or a goat. Every morning and every evening the priests make a burnt offering to God on behalf of the whole nation. On the Sabbath Day, they offer two animals in the evening and the morning. The sacrifice is given its name because the whole animal is burned. Its name in Hebrew means something like "It all goes up."

Apart from the sacrifices offered on behalf of the whole community, any individual Israelite who wishes to do so can make this sacrifice to God. This worshipper will offer it in view of the whole community. The scene can hardly be more dramatic. The worshipper chooses the best animal he can afford: a bull, a sheep, a goat or even a bird. It all depends on his financial situation. However, the animal must be without any blemish or disease. The worshipper is not expected to bring a second-rate offering to God.

The worshipper brings the animal to the door of the Tabernacle and explains the reason for the sacrifice. Many years later, when the Temple has been built by Solomon, the Temple choir would sing some psalms to accompany the offering of the sacrifice. After making his offering the worshipper lays his hands on the animal as an act of identifying himself with it. He kills the animal while the priests catch the blood of the sacrifice in a ritual bowl. The animal is skinned and dismembered. The worshipper offers each part of the animal in turn to a priest. He stands close by as the priest places each piece on the altar and he watches as the whole carcass, his sacrifice to God, is slowly consumed in the flames. The fact that the whole animal is offered in sacrifice can be seen as a picture of the worshipper's total dedication to God.

The burnt offering is a voluntary sacrifice. The worshipper chooses to make this sacrifice to God. It is costly, especially if a bull or a sheep is offered, for these animals have great value and are essential for the wellbeing and survival of the family.

The sacrifice of a burnt offering is also very public. The animal is brought to the door of the Tabernacle and sacrificed at the large altar which stands just inside the entrance. The ritual takes place in full view of anyone who cares to watch. The whole community will be aware of what is taking place and may ask themselves why the sacrifice is being made.

What's so important about the burnt offering?

Three phrases in Leviticus 1 help us to understand the primary intent behind the burnt offering. The worshipper is instructed to bring his offering to the tent of meeting *"so that it will be acceptable to the*

Lord' (verse 3). The aim of this sacrifice is to reconcile the worshipper to God. It opens the way for the worshipper to draw near to God without fear of condemnation. Paul rejoices that this is precisely what Jesus has done for us. He has reconciled us to God by the sacrifice of himself (2 Corinthians 5:18). We can now come boldly and confidently into the presence of God before whom we have full acceptance (Ephesians 3:12).

The second phrase, in verse 4, says that the purpose of the burnt offering is *"to make atonement for you."* The word used here can be understood in many different ways. The literal meaning of the Hebrew word is "to cover." So, this sacrifice acts as a covering over the sin or fault committed by the worshipper which is no longer exposed to view. The word is also used in the Old Testament to mean to pay a price or a ransom.

Pirates operating off the coast of Somalia are reported to board ships and kidnap their crew. They demand the payment of a ransom before the crew can be released. In the context of sacrifice, the imagery is that a price must be paid before the sin of the worshipper can be forgiven. In this case, the death of an animal is the price demanded and paid. The animal dies in place of the worshipper.

The third phrase which explains the meaning of the burnt offering appears in verse 9. There we read that the sacrifice is *"an aroma pleasing to the Lord."* The fragrance rising from the sacrifice has turned away God's anger. In the story of Noah, when God saw how wicked everyone was on earth and how evil their thoughts were all the time, he regretted that he had made human beings and his heart was deeply troubled. But after the flood, Noah built an altar and sacrificed burnt offerings. The Lord smelled the pleasing aroma and said: "Never again will I curse the ground because of humans" (Genesis 8:20ff.).

When we read about God being pleased by a fragrant aroma, we are describing God as if he acts and behaves just as we do. The only reason the Bible uses language like this is that we have no other than human words to describe what God is like, and at least it gives us some idea of what is happening here. Having said that, human language has limitations and is inadequate to describe God.

The fact that God can be pleased suggests that he can also be displeased by the way men and women behave. That is part of his nature. He will always be angry when people do wrong things. He will never be pleased with the evil that people do and will not ignore it. He cannot express approval of such behaviour; he must always express his disapproval. That is what the Bible means by his anger.

God's anger is a terrible thing. The Bible gives numerous examples of what may happen when God is angry. We only have to look at the punishment of Cain who was sent away from the presence of the Lord, or the destruction of the cities of Sodom and Gomorrah, or the disastrous episode of the golden calf. God is holy and he will always express his anger at what is unholy.

The worshipper who brings a burnt offering before the Lord does so because he is aware of the wrong things he has done. He feels a profound sense of guilt and knows that he stands condemned before God. But God has graciously provided a way for his anger to be averted through sacrifice. As blood is shed and the life of the animal is given, so the anger of God is averted. When Paul speaks of the death of Jesus on the cross, he writes: "Christ loved us and gave himself up for us as a fragrant offering and sacrifice to God" (Ephesians 5:2).

GIVING THANKS FOR DAILY BREAD (2:1-16)

The **grain offering** involves the offering of grain, usually of wheat or barley, ground into flour, together with oil and spices. These represent the basic ingredients of everyday food, and they are offered to God as an act of thanksgiving and in recognition of the people's dependence on his provision. Salt is added as a preservative and a reminder of the covenant (verse 13), for it is through obedience to the covenant that the people of Israel will be preserved from the corrupting influences of the surrounding cultures.

In this vein, yeast and honey are avoided (verse 11), for they are both viewed as symbols of corruption and fermentation. Jesus warns his disciples to beware of the leaven (yeast) of the Pharisees and Sadducees (Matthew 16:6). There are practical reasons too. Honey, in particular, will attract ants and other insects.

When Rosemary and I were living in rural Ethiopia, we saw how ants were attracted to anything that was sweet. We put a freshly baked cake in what we thought was an airtight tin but, when we opened the tin some time later, we found the cake crawling with ants. We shook out as many as we could but we still ate the cake. It was too precious to throw away. There were no supermarkets or patisseries where we lived! It helped us understand why God advised the Israelites not to add honey to their sacrifices.

PRAYING FOR BLESSINGS AND PEACE (3:1-17)

The Hebrew word for peace, *shalom,* means more than just an absence of war or anxiety. It carries the idea of wholeness, of total wellbeing. The **peace offering** is made to God by those who are grateful for blessings received or for specific answers to prayer. It can also be offered as a petition to God by those with a particular need. In the first chapter of 1 Samuel, a woman called Hannah goes with her husband to pray to the Lord for a child. The couple make a peace offering, both as an expression of thanksgiving and as a petition.

14

Unlike the burnt and grain offerings, the whole of this offering is not burnt. Part is offered to God; part is eaten by the priests; and the rest is consumed by the worshipper and his family. This sharing of the offering is an expression of fellowship with God and each other. It is a reminder of the meal that the seventy elders, including Moses, ate in the presence of God (Exodus 24:9–11).

In the New Testament, Paul reminds us that Christ has made peace by his blood on the cross (Romans 5:1). At the celebration of the Lord's Supper, we eat bread and wine together, symbolising both our communion with the Lord and with each other.

SEEKING CLEANSING AND RESTORATION (4:1 – 6:7)

Besides the burnt offering two other types of sacrifice deal with the effects of sin: the **sin offering** (Leviticus 4:1–5:13) and the **trespass offering** (Leviticus 5:14–6:7). It is not easy to differentiate between these sacrifices. Each one highlights a different aspect of the impact of sin. The burnt offering focuses primarily on the effect of sin on individuals and their relationship with God. The sin offering seems to emphasise the way sin affects the environment in which the Israelites live, while the trespass offering relates more particularly to the impact sin has on a person's relationship with his neighbours.

In the sin offering, there is a strong emphasis on the need to cleanse both the individual and his immediate location. The presence of sin causes the individual to feel unclean and guilty and the aim of this offering is to remove that sense of guilt and restore a sense of cleanliness. Similarly, when sin is committed in a certain place it can leave behind a sense of something evil and render that place unholy in God's sight. It suggests that the place needs to be cleansed and made holy and fit for God's presence. When we were living in Singapore, we realised that Chinese Christians were more aware of the presence of evil in a house if some crime had been committed there or idols had been worshipped. They would pray in each room to cleanse the whole place so God could return.

Cleansing is achieved through the shedding of blood, which brings assurance of forgiveness to the worshipper, and renewal and restoration to the environment. So, for example, in the Tabernacle, blood is smeared on the furniture and on the robes of the high priest to purify both the individual and the sanctuary.

John picks up this idea in his first letter: "If we claim to be without sin, we deceive ourselves and the truth is not in us. If we confess our sins, he is faithful and just and will forgive us our sins and purify us from all unrighteousness" (1 John 1:8ff.). Later in the Book of Revelation, John refers to those he sees in heaven dressed in robes of white who "have washed their robes and made them white in the blood of the Lamb" (Revelation 7:14), while Peter also alludes to this offering when he tells Christians that they have been "sprinkled with his blood" (1 Peter 1:2).

When a sin offering is brought to the altar, only a small part of the animal is consumed in the fire. The rest of the carcass is not burnt within the court of the Tabernacle. The thought behind this is that the sins of the people have been laid upon the sacrifice and it has to be symbolically removed from the camp lest it causes the place to be defiled. The priest has to take the carcass far away and destroy it outside the camp (Leviticus 4:12). That is the point picked up by the author of Hebrews who points out that just as the bodies of bulls offered as sin offerings are burnt outside the camp, so "Jesus also suffered outside the city gate to make the people holy through his own blood" (Hebrews 13:12).

In the trespass offering, which centres on the restoration of the relationship between the worshipper and his neighbour, there is a strong emphasis on restitution. Anything that has been taken or misappropriated must be restored and a further twenty per cent of the value added. In the gospels, Jesus tells his hearers that before they offer any gift to God, they should first put right any broken relationships. That is precisely what Zacchaeus does, once he is changed through his dynamic encounter with Jesus. He gives away half of his possessions and says he will pay back those he has cheated four times what he has taken (Luke 19:1–10).

ONE SACRIFICE FOR ALL TIME

The letter to the Hebrews makes it clear that none of the sacrifices can remove the consequences of sin: "It is impossible for the blood of bulls and goats to take away sins" (Hebrews 10:4). That is why the priests have to keep offering sacrifices day after day. The rituals bring a sense of forgiveness and cleansing, but they are not the basis on which God can forgive sins. They are a temporary currency that is valid at the time. It is like fifty-dollar bills or ten-pound notes which are accepted at their face value, but only because they represent a small amount of gold kept in Fort Knox or in the vaults of the Bank of England.

The value of the Old Testament sacrifices lies not in the sacrifices themselves, but in the fact that they point towards the perfect sacrifice that the Lord Jesus will offer for the sins of the world. "He is the atoning sacrifice for our sins, and not only for ours but also for the sins of the whole world" (1 John 2:2). "Day after day every priest stands and performs his religious duties; again and again he offers the same sacrifices, which can never take away sins. But when this priest had offered for all time one sacrifice for sins, he sat down at the right hand of God." (Hebrews 10:11–12)

As we read the New Testament, we see how the different categories of sacrifice described in Leviticus are pictures of the sacrifice of Jesus. The more we understand the significance and meaning of the sacrifices, the more we will understand what Jesus has achieved on our behalf. It may not be an exaggeration to say that we cannot fully appreciate the significance of the death of Jesus unless we understand the teaching of sacrifice in Leviticus. Perhaps there is no single picture in the Old Testament which portrays this more vividly than the burnt offering.

The New Testament frequently picks up the terms used in Leviticus 1 and applies them to Jesus. Jesus himself says: "For even the Son of Man did not come to be served, but to serve, and to give his life a ransom for many" (Mark 10:45). John writes in his first letter: "He [Jesus] is the atoning sacrifice for our sins" (1 John 2:2). Peter declares: "For you know that it was not with perishable things such as silver or gold that you were redeemed from the empty way of life handed down to you from your ancestors, but with the precious blood of Christ, a lamb without blemish or defect" (1 Peter 1:18–19).

When we think of the Lord Jesus, described in the New Testament as our sacrifice, we must see that there has been no sacrifice more willingly given, more costly or more public. Firstly, he gives himself willingly. He is the Good Shepherd who gives his life for the sheep. He has the power to lay his life down and power to take it again, but for our sake he chooses to die so that we may live forever (John 10).

Secondly, he pays the ultimate price for our salvation. He leaves the glory of heaven and becomes a human baby, born in an occupied country among a despised people into a poor family. During his trial and on the cross, he endures not only indescribable pain, but also the horror of being separated from his father as he bears the weight of human sin in his own body.

Thirdly, he dies in full public gaze. His cross is erected on a hill outside Jerusalem. People watch and mock him as he died. For two thousand years, the world has continued to look at the cross. Some

18

have sneered in ridicule, some have gazed in wonder, while millions have worshipped in adoration. Men and women have carved his death in stone or wood, painted it on canvas, and portrayed it in glass or in song.

The elaborate rituals of sacrifice in Leviticus speak volumes of the wonder of God's grace and testify to the depths of his love. Our God cares so much for us that he wants to restore our relationship with him after we have gone astray. He has sent his only son to die for us, and paid the price of our sins once and for all. Unlike the people of Israel, we do not have to follow all the minutiae of instructions and rituals to obtain forgiveness. However, like them, we still want to draw near to God to ask forgiveness, to bring our requests, and to express our thanks to him for all that he has done and continues to do for us. We can make our way to God's heart with boldness, confidence and joy through the perfect sacrifice of Jesus.

LEARNING TO PRAY

What can we learn from Leviticus 1–7 that will help us in our struggles with prayer? We can start by remembering that we are God's children, that he has chosen and adopted us into his family. All the instructions that God gave in these chapters were not given to people who were trying to establish their relationship with him but to those who had been chosen, rescued and adopted as his people. God wanted them to go on enjoying that relationship. The instructions on worship would maintain and deepen that relationship. In the same way, God wants us to continue to enjoy our relationship with him and for that relationship to develop and grow. He wants us to spend time in his presence, reflecting on his wonderful character and falling more deeply in love with him. Like the hymn writer Frederick Faber, we can reflect on who God is:

My God, how wonderful thou art,
thy majesty how bright!
How beautiful thy mercy seat,
in depths of burning light!

Wondrous are thine eternal years,
O everlasting Lord,
by holy angels day and night
unceasingly adored!

Secondly, we need to focus on God's forgiveness rather than our guilt. God provided such elaborate rituals to assure the people of their forgiveness. As for us, he has given his only son so that we can know that we too are forgiven, that there is no condemnation for those who are in Christ Jesus. While God is sad when we do wrong, he does not want us to dwell on our sins but on his love and forgiveness. We need to learn to bathe in the wonder of his forgiveness rather than feel sorry for ourselves because of our failures.

Thirdly, just as the Israelites regularly gave thank offerings of grain to God, we should make thanksgiving a major part of our regular prayer life. The Psalmist says: "Let us come before him with thanksgiving" (Psalm 95:2) and "Enter his gates with thanksgiving and his courts with praise" (Psalm 100:4). Paul tells the Christians in Philippi to make sure that every time of prayer time is accompanied by thanksgiving (Philippians 4:6). I must confess that most of my prayers are taken up with asking God for things rather than thanking him for all that he has done and continues to do. Before we ask for more, we should thank God for what we have already received. We should "count our blessings, name them one by one, and it will surprise us what the Lord has done."

Fourthly, as the people of Israel made peace offerings as an expression of the peace with God they enjoyed and as a request that they would continue to enjoy his blessings, so we pray that we may experience his grace and receive what we need. Because we are God's children, we are able to share everything with him, our concerns, hopes and fears. He knows all about them anyway. He knows us better than we know ourselves. Psalm 139 puts it very well: "You have searched me, Lord, and you know me. You know when I sit and when I rise; you perceive my thoughts from afar. You discern my going out and my lying down; you are familiar with all my ways. Before a word is on my tongue you, Lord, know it completely" (Psalm 139:1–4). Paul encourages us not to be anxious about anything, but in every situation, by prayer and petition, with thanksgiving, to present our requests to God. In the light of such encouragement, it is surprising that so often we do not take our concerns to the Lord but worry about them instead. Often the Lord is the last person we talk to about our worries.

Fifthly, note that the people of Israel spent two years at the foot of Mount Sinai, being taught and instructed by God through his servant Moses. We should probably spend more time reflecting on God's word and listening to his voice than we do in telling him all our needs. Jesus promises to do whatever we ask in his name, but we do not usually take the time to ask him first what is his will in any given situation. Like the prophet Habakkuk, we need sometimes just to be still, to wait and to listen.

Finally, we need to take appropriate action after we have prayed. If we have asked for forgiveness, we need to seek, by God's grace, not to repeat the same mistake. If we have thanked God for what he has done, we need to show our gratitude by the way we live. If we have made a request to God, we need to trust that he has listened and will respond appropriately. In the case of the trespass offering, the worshipper was required to repay any money he had taken from another or to recompense any who had been injured by his action. If we have listened to God and he has pointed out an action that we must take or an apology we should make to someone we have offended, we must be sure that we do so.

FOR PERSONAL REFLECTION

1. How would you define sin? What areas of your life would you include in your definition?

2. To the people of Israel, the offering of sacrifice served as a powerful reminder of the nature of God and the consequences of the wrong they had done. Their sin was so serious that only death could atone for their actions and restore them to a right relationship with God. Let us spend some time reflecting on the holiness of God and the seriousness of our sins.

3. Think about times when you have wronged another person and, subsequently, restored the relationship by putting right the wrong you had done. Can you think of other times when you failed to apologise or make appropriate reparation?

4. Reflect on passages in the New Testament which speak of the death of Jesus as a sacrifice offered willingly so that we might live (for example, Mark 10:45, Ephesians 5:2, 1 Peter 1:18, 1 John 2:2), and spend some time to worship him and express your thanks.

Chapter 2

A Life of Service

What do you do in your local church? Perhaps you lead a home group or teach in the Sunday school? Perhaps you are the church treasurer or sing in the choir? You may preach or be a worship leader. Perhaps you are one of those who use your gifts of administration, service, friendship, hospitality, or pastoral care. In 1 Corinthians 12, Paul describes the church as a body consisting of many members, who each have a critical role to play. He points out that while some people may be prominent in the fellowship, there are others who quietly make equally important contributions to the church.

In this chapter we look at some special individuals—the priests and Levites—and their work among the people of Israel. This group hold a very significant position in the community as those whose task it is to teach the people and lead them in worship. Today, we do not need priests who have the same role as that held by the priests in the Old Testament. What we do have, however, is a new kind of priesthood.

Leviticus 8–10

At eighty-three years of age, Aaron, often overshadowed by his more illustrious younger brother Moses, is given the job of his life. Together with his four sons, he is appointed to serve God as a priest (Exodus 28:1). As priests, Aaron and his sons will play an intermediary role between the Israelites and God, offering sacrifices on their behalf and blessing them in God's name. They are also called to lead the people in worship, to guide them when they have to make difficult decisions, to pray for them, and to teach them from God's word. In these respects, though not in all aspects of their role, it is possible to draw some parallels between the role of priests and the responsibilities of pastors or elders in churches today.

As we look at Leviticus 8–10, we will learn how priests are appointed, the significance of the clothes they wear, and the tasks they are given. We shall also look at the tragic account of what happens when they fail to carry out their role properly and behave inappropriately. Towards the end of the chapter, we will see how their priestly role as mediators is perfectly fulfilled in the Lord Jesus.

THE APPOINTMENT OF PRIESTS (8:1-31)

The priests, in particular the High Priest, play a crucial function in the life of the people of Israel. To be a priest is to occupy a position of great honour. Aaron, the first High Priest, is second only to Moses in authority. No one can presume to become a priest. No one can train to become one. All have to be **chosen** and appointed by God. That distinction belongs to Aaron and his descendants, and they serve as God's priests for life: "the priesthood shall be theirs by a statute forever" (Exodus 29:9).

Shortly after the call of Aaron and his sons to the priesthood, the tribe of Levi earns the honour of serving God through their action on Mount Sinai when many Israelites start to worship a golden calf and indulge in a sexual orgy (Exodus 32:25–29). The people are running wild, but the Levites rally around Moses to stand for God and restore order in the camp. Moses says to the Levites: "You have been set apart to the Lord today" (Exodus 32:29), and God appoints them to assist Aaron in his priestly duties. "They are to perform duties for him [Aaron] and for the whole community at the tent of meeting by doing the work of the tabernacle" (Numbers 3:7).

Once the priests have been called, they have to be **cleansed**. They are bathed, their clothes are washed, and a sacrifice is offered to cleanse them from sin (Leviticus 8:2–6). This is a reminder that the priests are the same as anybody else. They are not perfect human beings. They have faults and weaknesses. If they are to lead the people in worship and to draw near to a holy God on their behalf, it is necessary for them to be made clean.

The regalia of office

The priests have an elaborate wardrobe that is appropriate for their special duties. Aaron is **clothed** in special garments "to give him dignity and honour" (Exodus 28:2). A detailed description is given of the robes—made by skilled craftsmen—which Aaron wears as the High Priest. Each piece of clothing is highly symbolic and reflects his status and position as the intermediary between God and the people.

The tunic. First, he puts on a white linen tunic with a belt. This simple piece of clothing symbolises the truth that he can come into God's presence only because God has purified him from sin. He is regarded as being clean and righteous in the sight of God.

The robe. Next, over the tunic, Aaron wears a blue robe. It may be significant that the robe is the colour of the sky, for the priest is representing the God of heaven. The robe is decorated at its foot with bells and pomegranates. The people cannot always see the High Priest because a high fence surrounds the courtyard of the Tabernacle, and thick curtains hang at the entrance of the inner sanctuary. But they can hear the bells at the bottom of his robe and be assured that he is approaching God in worship and interceding on their behalf.

The ephod. On top of the robe, the High Priest wears a long jacket called an ephod (Leviticus 8:7). On the shoulders of the ephod are two stones, each engraved with the names of six of the twelve tribes of

Israel. As the High Priest goes into God's presence to intercede for the nation, he carries the names of those tribes on his shoulder, a symbolic picture of his prayer for them.

The breastplate. The next garment the High Priest wears is called the breastplate. It is like a large pouch, beautifully decorated on the outside with twelve precious and semi-precious stones, each stone representing one of the twelve tribes. Inside the pouch are two special stones called the Urim and the Thummim (Leviticus 8:8). The purpose of these stones is to provide guidance to the people when they are faced with an important decision. In seeking God's will, they go to the High Priest, who will then throw the two stones on the ground and decide God's will on the basis of how the stones fall.

No description is given of the stones themselves, but it has been suggested that they may have carried a positive symbol on one side and a negative symbol on the other. If both stones show the same symbol, clear guidance will have been given. If they show opposite symbols, the message will be indecisive with no guidance given. It may seem a strange system to discover God's guidance, but with the coming of the Holy Spirit at Pentecost the people of God no longer needed to use such means.

Today, as we discern God's will through prayer and the guidance of the Holy Spirit, the twin stones of the Urim and the Thummim are a reminder of God's promise to guide his people. The psalms encourage us to commit our way to God and trust that he will guide us as we do so (Psalm 37:5). The book of Acts gives some specific examples of how God guides Philip, Peter and Paul as they seek to share the good news with others (Acts 8, 10 and 16).

The turban. The final garment of the High Priest is a turban on his head (Leviticus 8:9). The Jewish historian Josephus records that it is twenty metres in length, but he is prone to exaggeration! The turban appears to have been a very long piece of material that is wound round the head. On the front of the turban is a golden plate on which are carved the words "holy to the Lord"—those who are called to lead the worship of God's people must themselves be holy.

After the High Priest has been called, cleansed and clothed, the final stage of his preparation is for him and his sons to be **consecrated** and ordained. This takes place through a series of rituals involving animal sacrifice and the anointing of each of the priests. They are anointed with the blood of a ram and with sacred oil reserved for this purpose (8:22–27, 30). They are anointed on the lobe of their right ear, the thumb of their right hand and the big toe of their right foot, indicating that they are to be dedicated to God in whatever they think, whatever they do, and wherever they go.

THE WORK OF PRIESTS (9: 1-24)

On the eighth day after the start of their consecration ceremony, Aaron and his sons begin their ministry by making sacrifices to God. That leads to a dramatic appearance of the glory of God, prompting an outburst of joy and worship from the people. The offering of sacrifices and the pronouncement of blessing are the primary functions of the priests, but there are other extremely important duties they have to fulfil (Leviticus 9:22–24).

One of these is to pray for the people. We have seen this symbolically represented by the fact that the High Priest carries the names of the tribes on his shoulders when he goes into the presence of God. The semi-precious stones on his breastplate show that he stands before God as the representative of each of the twelve tribes, and he is offering prayers for them.

In Exodus 19, Moses tells the people of Israel that they will become a kingdom of priests. They have come to know the true God and part of their calling is to share their knowledge of God with the rest of the world through witness and intercession. Subsequently, during the eight days of celebration at the annual feast of Tabernacles in Jerusalem, it is customary to offer seventy sacrifices, one for each of the nations of the known world. Peter, in his first letter, describes believers as belonging to a holy priesthood (1 Peter 2:5). We too are called to fulfil that priestly calling by witnessing to and praying for the nations of the world.

Another essential role of the priests is to teach the people the word of God. That responsibility is stated clearly in the closing blessing of Moses to the tribes in Deuteronomy 33. He says that the tribe of Levi "watched over your word and guarded your covenant. He teaches your precepts to Jacob and your law to Israel" (Deuteronomy 33:9–10). Later in the Old Testament, Ezra, described as a priest and teacher of the Law of the God of heaven (Ezra 7:12), provides us with a model of what a priest is supposed to do. He "devoted himself to the study and observance of the law of the Lord, and to teaching its decrees and laws in Israel" (Ezra 7:10). Nehemiah is just as devoted to teaching God's word; he gathers the whole population of Jerusalem and reads to them from the Bible for a whole day—with short stops for meals (Nehemiah 8).

WHEN THINGS GO WRONG (10: 1-20)

In 1989, televangelist Jim Bakker was sentenced to five years in prison on twenty-four counts of fraud and conspiracy after misappropriating funds from followers for his own use. In October 2015, Bishop Peter Ball, formerly Bishop of Gloucester, was sentenced to thirty-two months' imprisonment for misconduct in public office and indecent assault after admitting to the abuse of eighteen young men over a period of fifteen years from 1977 to

1992. Christians are shocked by such headlines and the witness of the worldwide church is seriously damaged. Those who are called to positions of trust and leadership among God's people are expected to be a model of godly living. Sadly, two of Aaron's sons fail to set such an example with tragic consequence.

One may have thought that his sons will have taken great care to carry out their responsibilities and to live lives that befitted their calling. Sadly, two of them do not. In Leviticus 10, Nadab and Abihu do not honour God in the way they conduct worship and perform sacrifices. It is not clear from the text what is the exact nature of their sin. They offer what is described as unauthorised fire before the Lord (10:1). They fail to recognise that God is holy and that his word must be obeyed in its entirety. They cannot choose to do only the things they want to. It is possible that they start doing rituals which are their father's prerogative to perform. It also seems likely that they are drunk at the time, since a few verses later in the chapter, God tells Aaron: "You and your sons are not to drink wine or other fermented drink whenever you go into the tent of meeting, or you will die."

Whatever the nature of their wrongdoing, the consequences are catastrophic: "So fire came out from the presence of the Lord and consumed them, and they died before the Lord" (10:2). It is hard to understand such a dreadful punishment, but it is an unforgettable lesson for those who exercise leadership among God's people and lead them in worship. James warns: "Not many of you should become teachers, my fellow believers, because you know that we who teach will be judged more strictly" (James 3:1). Moses himself will learn the same painful lesson when he refuses to trust God and loses his temper with the crowd who are constantly criticising him (Numbers 20). Spiritual leaders must lead holy lives, be examples of obedience, and show deep reverence for God and his word.

THE PERFECT HIGH PRIEST

The Levitical priesthood brings into sharp focus for us the uniqueness of Jesus as a High Priest. As prestigious as the office of High Priest is in Old Testament times, the undeniable fact is that the high priests are sinful like the people they represent. They have to bring sin offerings for themselves first before they can do so for anybody else. In the New Testament, however, there The writer of the letter to the Hebrews draws a comparison between Jesus and the Levitical priesthood. He describes Jesus: "Such a high priest truly meets our need—one who is holy, blameless, pure, set apart from sinners, exalted above the heavens. Unlike other high priests, he does not need to offer sacrifices day after day, first for his own sins, and then for the sins of the people. He sacrificed for their sins once for all when he offered himself" (Hebrews 7:26–27).

In the course of time, Aaron and all the others who serve as High Priests die. They have to transfer the priesthood to someone else. They can only serve as priests and offer sacrifices for the nation merely for the limited period of their lives. Even then, their numerous sacrifices are not enough to cover the continuing sins of all the people. The next priests had to continue to make sacrifices too, so it is a never-ending cycle of sacrifices. By contrast, Jesus does not have to die. He is alive forever to serve as our High Priest. "Therefore, he is able to save completely those who come to God through him, because he always lives to intercede for them" (Hebrews 7:25).

Jesus is also a perfect High Priest because he has lived as a human being. "For this reason he had to be made like them, fully human in every way, in order that he might become a merciful and faithful high priest in service to God, and that he might make atonement for the sins of the people" (Hebrews 2:17). And being fully human, Jesus knows what it is like to face temptations: "For we do not have a high priest who is unable to empathize with our weaknesses, but we have one who has been tempted in every way, just as we are—yet he did not sin" (Hebrews 4:15).

We all face temptations, and constantly struggle with them. Sometimes we are confronted with a temptation that is so strong it almost overwhelms us. The temptations we face may not be the same as those Jesus faced. As the Son of God, he is tempted to use his supernatural powers for his own ends, to establish his universal kingdom and gain universal admiration. In some ways these temptations are greater than those we face. But because he has been tempted, Jesus understands what a battle it can be and can understand and sympathise with us in our spiritual battles. This gives us the assurance not to waver in our faith in trying times: "Let us then approach God's throne of grace with confidence, so that we may receive mercy and find grace to help us in our time of need (Hebrews 4:16).

When Rosemary and I were living in Ethiopia, we knew a number of those who were priests in the Ethiopian Orthodox Church. In their tradition they offered the mass every day as a sacrifice for sin. Once, a group of Orthodox priests were reading through the letter to the Hebrews when they came across these verses: "And every priest stands daily at his service, offering repeatedly the same sacrifices, which can never take away sins. But when Christ had offered for all time a single sacrifice for sins, he sat down at the right hand of God, waiting from that time until his enemies should be made a footstool for his feet. For by a single offering he has perfected for all time those who are being sanctified" (Hebrews 10:11–14, ESV). The priests could hardly believe what they had read and became so excited. While they were happy still to lead worship in their churches, they knew that they did not need to offer anything to God to be forgiven or be made acceptable to him. They were forgiven already, and forever.

A KINGDOM OF PRIESTS

In his letter to the Ephesians, Paul teaches that Christ has appointed apostles, prophets, evangelists, pastors and teachers, so that God's people can be built up in their faith and be equipped for works of service (Ephesians 4:11). None of those appointed to these offices are to function in the same way that priests did in the Old Testament, for such priestly service is no longer necessary. They are, however, to take great care to serve Christ and his church.

Peter encourages those who are elders in the church to be good shepherds of God's flock and to set a good example for others to follow (1 Peter 5:1-4). Those who are in positions of leadership face numerous pressures. They may feel the weight of expectations or find the load of pastoral care, administration and preaching almost intolerable. At the same time, they face the same temptations as any other believer. We need to do all we can to support them and to pray that God will sustain them and enable them to live holy lives.

In his first letter, Peter also says something extraordinary to believers scattered across the Roman Empire. He tells them that they are "a chosen people, a royal priesthood" (1 Peter 2:9). This royal priesthood is a priesthood to which all Christians belong. Like believers in the early church we have been **chosen** by God to become his children and we have all been appointed to serve our king as priests. We too are given the responsibility to pray for the nations and to tell people about God.

But first, just like the High Priest, we need to be **cleansed** from our sin. We are so thankful that Jesus has died in our place so that we can be forgiven. Now in heaven he represents us before the face of God, the throne of grace and the judgement seat. Paul writes of these glorious truths: "Who will bring any charge against those whom God has chosen? It is God who justifies. Who then is the one who condemns? No one. Christ Jesus who died—more than that, who was raised to life—is at the right hand of God and is also interceding for us" (Romans 8:33–34).

Secondly, Jesus has made it possible for us to serve him and to stand unashamed in God's presence. Just as the High Priest was clothed with a white tunic, so God has **clothed** those who trust in him with the robe of righteousness (Isaiah 61:10). Jesus tells a parable about the kingdom of heaven, where one of the guests is not wearing an appropriate wedding garment. When the king sees him, he gets angry and throws the man out of the wedding banquet. It is customary at that time for the host to provide a wedding garment for guests to wear. Apparently, this man has refused to wear it, preferring instead to wear his own clothes. The point that Jesus makes is that all are welcome into the kingdom of heaven, no matter where they come from or what they have done, but they must come on God's terms. They must not rely on their own goodness, thinking that they are good enough as they are. They must understand that their lives appear as filthy rags in God's sight, that they can only come as sinners into his presence. But God is willing to forgive them and give them something appropriate to wear, a new white robe which demonstrates that they are now regarded as being righteous in God's sight.

Thirdly, after we have been cleansed from our sin and clothed with a robe of righteousness, we are called to be **consecrated** to God's service. Just as the priests were anointed on their right ear, their right hand and their right foot as a sign that they were to be dedicated to God in every part of their lives, every follower of Christ is called to demonstrate a similar dedication to God.

It is sometimes assumed that whereas we expect ministers or missionaries to be totally committed to Christ and to lead impeccable lives, we do not need to apply the same standards to ourselves. The call to holiness, to dedication to Christ, to faithful service and witness, is the same for every member of the church family, whether we do the washing up or preach sermons. None of us are called to fulfil all the functions of the priests as described in Leviticus, but we are called through the grace of God. We are all cleansed through the blood of Christ; we are all clothed with his righteousness. In everything we think and say and do, we are to be consecrated to his service. God's people today are called to be a holy priesthood.

Finally, just as the priests and Levites were called to fulfil a particular role among God's people, so every Christians is called to serve God and to play our part in the life of the fellowship to which we belong. Some are given the particular responsibilities of leaders, being called to devote their time to leading worship, pastoring and teaching God's people. Others are called to use their gifts in the service of Christ in another country. Each believer needs to be open to the possibility God may call them to such service. Many Christians serve in a voluntary capacity as elders, home group leaders or Sunday school teachers. But every Christian belongs to the royal priesthood and every Christian is called to serve the king.

FOR PERSONAL REFLECTION

What are your areas of responsibility or ministry within your church? To what extent do you view those as a chore or a privilege? How much time and effort do you put into the preparation and carrying out of those responsibilities? In what ways could you improve on how you do things?

1. The priests were anointed for service. How earnestly do you seek God's anointing for the ministry in which you are involved? How far has reliance on natural gifts, training courses, communication skills or the use of modern technology replaced our sense of dependence on God as we seek to serve him?

2. What does it mean to you to belong to a priesthood of all believers? What difference does it make to your life and your relationship with others?

Chapter 3

A Healthy Life

God is not just interested in our prayers and the role we play in our local church. He is concerned with every aspect of our lives, and that includes our physical wellbeing as well as our spiritual health. It may come as something of surprise that God wants to guide his people on what they eat as well as how they keep fit. But like any loving parent, he wishes to protect his children from illness, disease and accident. He does this through a national health programme outlined in Leviticus 11–16, which covers such topics as childbirth and maternity care, medical diagnosis, infections, quarantine and public hygiene. The section concludes with a description of the Day of Atonement, when the people of God are cleansed from everything— spiritual and physical—that may harm them or pollute their lives.

God's Public Health Programme (Leviticus 11–16)

The coronavirus pandemic of 2020 spread so rapidly it created a global medical crisis within a few weeks. It was a highly infectious respiratory disease, and spread easily as people travelled from country to country. To make matters worse, those who were infected but showed no signs of infection were totally unaware they were passing on the disease to others. Most nations were not prepared to handle such a crisis and were ill-equipped to cope with the rapidly evolving situation. Often the action they took was too little and too late. Some cancelled all flights and closed their borders in an attempt to stem the infection. Some imposed a lockdown on certain regions of their country or on their whole population.

Many introduced test-and-trace programmes to identify those who were sick and follow up those who had been in recent contact with them. In England, any who showed symptoms of the disease were at first required to self-isolate for seven, then ten, days, and those who had met with them recently, for fourteen days. People were told to wash their hands frequently and thoroughly. In the UK, residents were told to stay in their homes and only go outside when it was necessary to buy food or medication. The elderly and those with serious medical conditions were told they must not venture out at all. Even those who did go outside were recommended to wear face masks and to maintain a social distance of two metres.

The impact of this pandemic made governments realise afresh their responsibility to care for the health and the wellbeing of their people. It was their duty not only to oversee the adequate provision of healthcare, but also to anticipate and prepare for medical crises that may appear at any time. These governments can take a leaf out of God's handbook on public healthcare. Leviticus 11–16 show how much God cares for the health and wellbeing of his people. He is not just interested in their spiritual needs, but he also wants them to enjoy good health and long life. He is concerned that his people have a safe and wholesome diet, and are protected against eating contaminated food which might make them ill. He wants mothers who have given birth to receive adequate postnatal care, and have plenty of time to regain their strength. In these chapters God also prescribes an extensive programme for the detection and treatment of disease.

A SAFE DIET IN A HOT CLIMATE (11: 1-47)

In recent years billions of pounds have been spent by people who are passionate about finding the right diet to keep them healthy and happy. They consult dieticians, register for expensive courses and read everything they can find on how to eat healthily. Some seek to follow a balanced diet and take care to avoid white bread, sweet drinks and pizzas. Others opt for a vegetarian diet or even a vegan one, completely avoiding meat, fish, eggs and dairy products. The provision of dietary courses and the manufacture of dietary products have become a huge industry. According to a survey conducted in the US in 2017, the weight loss market in the country was worth US$66 billion, while apparently in Britain, according to Juliette Kellow, a leading dietician, women have spent more than £25,000 each on dieting over a lifetime, in their attempts to lose weight.

The proverb "You are what you eat" reflects the common conviction that the food we consume directly impacts our health. It affects our weight, energy levels, moods and reaction to stress. In most developed countries, there is an almost unlimited selection of food to eat. People are able to decide for themselves how much and what they eat. At the time of Moses, however, there was not the same choice; nor were there the same methods of preservation. There were no cookbooks or TV shows on how to cook safely in a desert.

When we look at the list of permitted and forbidden food in Leviticus 11, it may seem strange to us that some kinds of food are allowed, while others are regarded as unclean. What is the basis for the distinction? It helps for us to remember that the main purpose of this chapter is to give people, who are mostly illiterate, instructions on safe and nutritious eating while they are wandering around for forty years in the Negev.

Firstly, it is intended as a simple guide, which even a child can remember. The people are only allowed to eat the meat of animals that chew the cud and have cleft hooves. They are allowed to eat cows, sheep or goats, but not rabbits, camels or pigs. They can eat any kind of fish with fins and scales but must avoid anything that live in the water without those features. All winged insects are considered unclean except those that can hop.

Secondly, it is a safety guide, warning the people not to eat anything which may pass on disease, such as birds of prey or scavengers, or anything which may make them ill, such as pork or shellfish, in a hot climate where they have no refrigerators. Thus, they can eat herring, pike, trout, bass, haddock, cod and sardines, but not oysters, crabs, lobsters and shrimps.

While it is not possible to give a complete rationale for why types of food were permitted and others were not, we can observe that many of the edible crustacea feed on decaying flesh and can readily transmit infection. Even today, care needs to be taken to prevent food poisoning from shellfish, such as oysters, by ensuring that they are as fresh as possible, and purchased from a reputable merchant who stores them in appropriately chilled, sanitary conditions.

While the Israelites can eat doves, chickens, ducks, turkeys and pigeons, they are not allowed to eat eagles, owls, hawk, cuckoos, vultures or members of the crow family. Again, it may be difficult to discern the rationale behind these instructions. It is true, however, that birds of prey feed off carrion, the putrefying flesh of dead animals, as do the carrion crow and other members of the crow family. They are more likely to pass on disease than those birds which only eat seeds or berries. In the light of the discovery that bats have provided a refuge for some of the most lethal viruses known, including those that cause Ebola and SARS, and that many health experts believe the new strain of coronavirus most likely originated in bats, it is significant to note that bats are excluded from the diet of the people of Israel.

Thirdly, the guide given to the community in the desert is intended to provide a nutritious diet. Interestingly, it includes locusts, crickets and grasshoppers. People in the West are not particularly attracted to eating these but, in some cultures, they are viewed as delicacies. According to an article in *The Daily Telegraph* published in the UK in June 2008: "The bugs are rich in protein and minerals and are lower in cholesterol than beef or pork...Grasshoppers have 20 grams of protein and just 6 g of fat per 100g while fire ants have 13.9g of protein and 3.5g of fat. Crickets are sources of iron, zinc and calcium."

But there may further significance in the dietary rules set down in Leviticus 11. Food is a reflection of a particular culture or society. French cuisine is very different from Italian or Greek food. Indians, Thai, Chinese and Malays have developed differing styles of cooking, which in turn are marks of their distinct culture. The people of Israel inevitably develop their own recipes as they live in the desert and then move into the fertile land of Canaan. The food they eat is a mark of their national identity, and God calls his people to be distinct. "You shall be holy," God said. That means they are to be different not only in their pattern of worship but also in the way they live, and even in the food they eat. The food laws they are given marked them out as being a distinct people.

After entering the Promised Land, they continue to observe these laws, which remain in the culture of the Jewish people for thousands of years. Food that they are permitted to eat is said to be *kosher*, while food that is forbidden is regarded as unclean. Traditionally, Jewish people believe that eating unclean food will make them unclean in the sight of God.

These customs are similarly observed by Jesus and his disciples, although he declares that what you eat does not make you clean or unclean in the eyes of God. It is not the food that defiles but what comes out of the heart. Jesus says: "Don't you see that nothing that enters a person from the outside can defile them? For it doesn't go into their heart but into their stomach, and then out of the body" (Mark 7:18–19).

In saying this, Jesus declares all foods clean. Later, this becomes the source of a major problem in the early church because as long as Jewish Christians observe these kosher laws, they are unable to eat a fellowship meal with Gentile Christians who do not observe them. One solution is for the Gentile Christians to follow the same rules as well, but that will mean laying an unnecessary burden on them. Jesus has already made it clear that all types of food are clean and eating food that is not kosher does not threaten a person's salvation. While this is certainly good news for those Christians who love their bacon or their prawns, Leviticus 11 is a healthy reminder that God is concerned with what we eat.

CARE FOR NEW MUMS (12: 1-1-8)

In today's world, most countries have comprehensive postnatal care programmes to promote the welfare of the mother and her baby. These include advice on breastfeeding, washing, health and hygiene, and ensuring that the new mother has adequate time to rest and recuperate. The instructions given in Leviticus 12 aim to provide the Israelite mother with good postnatal care, ensuring that she recovers well after childbirth before assuming her full role as a wife and mother. That sounds like admirable advice, which provides time for the mother to recuperate and have respite from the attentions of her husband.

The period of convalescence concludes with a purification ceremony to allow the mother to have a medical check-up. The question then arises as to why a woman needs to be purified. In the context, it is not childbirth or the act of sexual intercourse but the loss of blood that makes the ritual purification necessary. Later in Leviticus we learn that blood symbolises life (17:11). When there is blood loss, a person's life is, to some extent, under threat. The body is not whole or as it should be. Having a baby in any culture comes with the risk of complications, but it is particularly so in the ancient world which lacks the advanced medical treatment available today.

Though the need for purification implies that there is something not quite right, the new mother herself has not done anything wrong. The uncleanness that is implied is not moral but ritual. After giving birth the woman is not yet completely healthy and so cannot participate in public worship. When fully well, she will be able to come again into God's house, and then atonement is made for her. This is a reminder that we are sinful people and constantly need God's cleansing and forgiveness as we come into his presence.

What may be puzzling from the text is that a mother who has a baby girl should be given twice as long for this period of purification and recuperation (12:3–5). This may reflect a lower value placed on daughters rather than sons in ancient Israelite culture. It has been suggested that the mother may have been disappointed that she has had a girl rather than a boy, and need more time to get over her sadness. Other commentators point out that the baby girl has the potential as a future mother of giving life, and therefore the event of her birth is treated as more special and requires a longer period of celebration. It is certainly true that women in Israel enjoy many rights and privileges that are not available to women in surrounding cultures. They have the same access to the sanctuary, and the sacrifice they are required to offer is the same whether they have a girl or a boy. Whatever may be the case, we can rejoice that the New Testament makes it abundantly clear that in Christ there is no distinction between male and female, and both approach God on the basis of the shed blood of Jesus (Galatians 3:28).

A CLINIC IN THE DESERT (13:1 – 15: 33)

By July 2020, more than seven million people have been infected by the coronavirus and more than 600,000 are known to have died. The US, UK, Spain, Italy and Brazil are among the countries most severely affected. People are surprised by the incredible speed this hidden plague spread from one person to another, and every possible means has been employed in many countries to control the spread of infection and bring the disease under control.

The people in Old Testament times are aware of how easily disease can be passed from one person to another, and how important it is to take urgent steps to limit the contagion. Leviticus 13–15 deal with these issues, providing advice for the diagnosis and treatment of infectious disease, and instructions on the steps taken to isolate those who are ill and prevent the spread of infection.

There is a list of infectious skin diseases in chapter 13. Some versions of the Bible refer to many of them as leprosy, but the symptoms described do not match what we understand today as leprosy. It would seem that a number of different diseases, characterised by spots, rashes or swellings, are described here.

It is the priests' duty to examine those who have developed some new disturbing symptoms, to apply tests and prescribe appropriate treatment. If there is uncertainty as to the nature of the disease, they will put the patient into isolation for seven days to observe any developments that may assist them in their diagnosis. If, at the end of that period, they decide there is nothing to worry about, they will allow the patient to return home. If they conclude that the patient is suffering from something serious, and possibly a contagious disease, they will put the person in strict quarantine until he or she completely recovers. Those infected with a serious disease are no longer able to take part in the life or worship of the people of God.

It is not only people who can be infected and, in turn, infect others. It is also recognised that clothes or walls can be a source of infection. Reference is made to the appearance of mould or fungus in woollen, linen and leather clothing in Leviticus 13:47–52. Such clothing can pass on disease to others in the community and make them and the whole community unholy or imperfect in the eyes of God. Infected garments have to be examined over a period of time and if there is persistent mould, they must be burnt.

In the New Testament a parallel is often drawn between the impact of disease in the life of the individual and the impact of sin. Just as disease makes people less than perfect or whole in the sight of God, and separates them from others, so sin has the same effect. In Ephesians, Paul talks about the impact of sin on their lives: "Remember that at that time you were separate from Christ, excluded from citizenship in Israel and foreigners to the covenants of the promise, without hope and without God in the world" (Ephesians 2:12).

Paul goes on to remind the Christians in Ephesus how they have been forgiven and cleansed through the cross: "But now in Christ Jesus you who once were far away have been brought near by the blood of Christ" (2:13). In the same way, the book of Leviticus describes how those who have been made unclean through disease can be made clean again and restored to the community. Chapter 14 goes into considerable detail in describing the various stages by which a person, after a period of quarantine and treatment, can be re-examined, cleansed and restored to the community.

Leviticus 15 deals with sexual cleanliness, and gives the example of a man with an unusual body discharge. This probably refers to gonorrhoea. Such a man is regarded as unclean and his uncleanness can be transmitted to others. Once his condition clears up, he is required to wait for seven days before being regarded as clean again.

After the emission of semen during normal sexual activity, the man is considered unclean until the evening, following which he has to wash himself. By contrast, a woman goes through a period of seven days during menstruation when she is regarded as unclean.

It is important to note again that there is no implication that there is anything wrong or dirty about sexual intercourse. That is a serious misunderstanding promulgated in some quarters of the Christian church. While these instructions do place some restraint on sexual activity, there is no inference either here or anywhere else in Scripture that intercourse is sinful. On the contrary, it is part of the glorious and perfect design of God our Creator that men and women should demonstrate their love for each other through their bodies.

The instructions given in Leviticus 11–15 may seem like a rather complicated set of laws and rituals and it is important not to get too bogged down in the details. The emphasis of these chapters is to show how our loving heavenly father is interested in every part of our lives. He is concerned for the wellbeing of mothers and babies, and the provision of appropriate medical care to those who are sick. At the same time, he is equally concerned with our physical, emotional and spiritual wellbeing. He treats us as whole beings. So the next chapter, Leviticus 16, brings assurance to the people that they can be made clean not only in their bodies but also in their hearts. They can be purified from disease and from anything which separated them from the God who loved them.

A DAY OF CLEANSING (16:1-34)

The coronavirus pandemic not only brought serious illness and death to many, but it also increased levels of stress and anxiety in many homes across the world. Uncertainty about the future, separation from loved ones, and the constant overload of bad news in the media increased those anxiety levels. Being in lockdown and

45

unable to continue with their regular work, many discovered they had time to reflect on their lives. For some this sparked an unhealthy level of introspection. Some became depressed as they thought about things they had done in the past or things they had failed to do. It is possible to worry about the past to the point where you make yourself physically ill. According to an old saying, you can worry yourself sick. Guilt is a powerful emotion which can destroy our inner peace and seriously affect our health.

In Matthew's gospel, before Jesus heals a paralysed man, he says to him: "Your sins are forgiven" (9:2). Jesus knows human beings need healing from disease and from the sickness of sin. He also realises that sickness can be exacerbated through feelings of guilt. He recognises the connection between the two and will often point out that it is the latter that is the more serious condition from which people need healing.

The Day of Atonement (Yom Kippur), described in Leviticus 16, follows the five chapters where God provides instructions for maintaining the physical health and wellbeing of his people. He now prescribes an annual ceremony which demonstrates the same principle that Jesus will exemplify when he heals the paralysed man, that God is concerned for his people to be whole in body and spirit. On this holy day, the High Priest is allowed to enter the Holy of Holies at the heart of the Tabernacle (16:2). This is the only day in the year when he is permitted to go into the very presence of the holy God. There he will offer sacrifice for the sins of all the people and through that sacrifice bring to the whole nation assurance of forgiveness and freedom from guilt.

The Day of Atonement is still regarded as the holiest day in the year for Jewish people. It is observed by Jews all over the world through prayer, fasting and public confession of sin. All the prohibitions regarding work on the Sabbath apply equally to this day, which is regarded as "the Sabbath of Sabbaths." There is no longer a tabernacle or a temple in which Jews can offer sacrifice, so atonement is sought through repentance for one's own sins and the sins of the community. The devout worshipper fasts for twenty-five hours, spends all day in the synagogue, and wears a white robe as a symbol of purity.

During the sacred ceremony described in Leviticus 16, the High Priest takes part in ceremonial washing before offering the sacrifice of a bull for himself and his family. He then chooses two goats. He sacrifices one as a sin offering for the whole nation, taking some of its shed blood into God's presence. He lays his hands on the head of the second goat and confesses over it all the sins of the people. After this, the goat is driven away into the desert, "bearing all their iniquities into a solitary land" (verse 22). God's desire for his people is that they are completely whole, in their physical bodies, in their hearts, and in their relation to himself.

While this ceremony brings temporary assurance of forgiveness to the people of Israel, it is strange that the second goat is only sent away rather than sacrificed. It can give the impression that the sins of the people have not been completely wiped out. Whether or not it is legitimate to draw such a conclusion, for many Jewish people, the observance of this day, the penitence, the good deeds and the charitable acts do not bring complete assurance of forgiveness. While many Jews may feel clean and forgiven and believe God understands and forgives them, others lack any such certainty. When a very devout Jewish neighbour, who had faithfully observed the twenty-five-hour fast of Yom Kippur, was asked whether he felt forgiven, he replied: "I hope so."

The complete assurance of forgiveness, however, can be received through Jesus. The writers of the New Testament frequently refer to the ceremonies of the Day of Atonement when they speak of the death of Jesus and, in particular, use the illustration of the scapegoat that is sent away bearing the sins of the nation. Paul explains: "God made him who had no sin to be sin for us, so that in him we might become the righteousness of God" (2 Corinthians 5:21). Peter says that Jesus "bore our sins in his body on the cross" (1 Peter 2:24). The writer to the Hebrews also reminds us: "It is impossible for the blood of bulls and goats to take away sins" (Hebrews 10:4). Ultimately it is only the sacrifice of Jesus, the Lamb of God that can take away sin.

FOR PERSONAL REFLECTION

1. During the coronavirus pandemic, people all over the world were deeply grateful to the doctors and nurses who showed such dedication in caring for those who became ill. In Britain the public gave those who worked for the National Health Service a round of applause every Thursday evening. How much do you appreciate those who look after your heath? How often do you pause to thank God that he cares for you?

2. Paul reminds us that we are stewards of our bodies, which are the temple of the Holy Spirit, and therefore we should glorify God in our bodies (1 Corinthians 6:19ff.). Do you see your body as the "temple of the Holy Spirit?" Do you honour God with your body by the way you treat it through food and exercise? In what ways do you seek to keep fit and well? How careful are you about what you eat? How regularly do you take exercise? How much care do you take to maintain good standards of hygiene and to avoid infection?

3. A lady was told by a priest that she had committed the unforgiveable sin. For years she lived with the terrible burden that God would never forgive her, but one day a friend told her that Jesus had died for all her sins and she could be forgiven. Are there any areas in your life where you still have

a lingering sense of guilt and are not sure that you have been forgiven and cleansed? Remember that Jesus died in our place so that we might know we are completely forgiven. Spend some time reflecting on things you have done in the past and things that you have failed to do. Thank God that though your sins are as scarlet, they will be as white as snow (Isaiah 1:18).

Chapter 4

A Holy Life

Talk the talk—that is the thrust of a book called 'Consistent Christianity' written a number of years ago by Dr Michael Griffiths, who served as General Director of OMF International and Principal of London Bible College. He pointed out that Christians should practise what they preach, that their behaviour should match up to their beliefs, and that in every area of their lives they should live in a way that is consistent with biblical teaching.

This is the message for the people of God in the closing section of Leviticus. God wishes his people to reflect his character in their attitudes and behaviour. This is as true for us today as it was for the people of Israel. He wants us to be exemplary in our personal lives, in our sexual behaviour and in the way we relate to our neighbours. He calls us to care for those less fortunate than ourselves and to play an active role in the life of our local community. He also wants us to have times to rest and celebrate, and to use those occasions not to have wild parties but to thank him for all that he has done for us. So in Leviticus 17–27 he provides a handbook on how to live as the people of God.

Leviticus 17–27

Time and again God calls his people to be like him: "You are to be holy to me because I, the Lord, am holy, and I have set you apart from the nations to be my own from the peoples, that you should be mine" (Leviticus 20:26). The word which is translated "holy" in our Bibles means to be distinct, to be set apart, to be different from anything else. The Bible says that God is holy, because he is distinct and set apart from all his creatures. He is perfect in everything he does and everything he says. He is free from all moral impurity or sin, and is therefore morally perfect.

God wants the people of Israel whom he has adopted as his family to reflect his character. He calls them to be holy, to be different from those around them. The closing chapters of Leviticus show them how to do this by providing them with instructions for daily living. Here is a practical guide to holiness, which reflects God's concern with every part of their lives: family life, business, finance, holidays, security and social welfare.

SEXUAL PURITY (18: 1-30)

Generations of Israelites have been accustomed to life in Egypt. But after God brings the people out of slavery, he commands them to live by his standards (Leviticus 18:1–5). Called to be holy in their moral behaviour, they are not to behave like the Egyptians or the people who live in Canaan. In other cultures in the Ancient Near East at that time incest was widely practised. Marriage between brothers and sisters, parents and children, was common in ancient Egypt among royalty and noble families. Since these elites were the representatives of the divine on earth, they were often privileged to do what was forbidden to members of ordinary families, in order to preserve the purity of their royal or divine blood.

Leviticus 18 sets out a list of relationships within which marriage is forbidden. It is important to remember that these laws are laid down as God's command and do not owe their origin to mere social convenience. In our contemporary world incest is rightly viewed as one of the most heinous forms of child abuse.

The practice of a man marrying his wife's sister, while his wife is still alive, is forbidden. The story of Jacob's marriage to two sisters, Leah and then Rachel, demonstrates the potential consequences of ignoring this law (Genesis 29–30). Jacob falls in love with Rachel, the younger and prettier sister, and wants to marry her. The girls' father, Laban, decides Jacob must marry the older sister first and only allows him to marry Rachel as a second wife. So, Jacob has two wives, but the tragedy of the situation is that Jacob clearly loves Rachel much more than Leah. Leah knows she is loved less and desperately tries to win her husband's affection by giving him four healthy sons, while Rachel is unable initially to have children. Both wives are equally unhappy. Leah has children but is not loved. Rachel is loved but has no children for many years. It is not difficult to imagine the unhappiness and tension in the family.

There is no similar list in the New Testament detailing whom you could or could not marry, but the followers of Jesus are encouraged to be pure in everything they do (Philippians 2:5). Paul encourages believers to "put to death, therefore, whatever belongs to your earthly nature: sexual immorality, impurity, lust, evil desires and greed, which is idolatry" (Colossians 3:5). Christians are to be radically different in their sexual conduct from those around them. They are not to accept the standards of the world. This represents one of the greatest challenges for Christians today, where standards of moral behaviour are based on the subjective feelings and preferences of the individual rather than the objective standards of God's word.

The latter part of Leviticus 18 deals with several forbidden sexual practices, including adultery, same-sex relationships and bestiality. The prohibition of adultery is enforced by Jesus (Matthew 5:27–30) as well as the teaching of the early church. Biblical passages such as Romans 13:9, Galatians 5:19 and Hebrews 13:4 also make it clear that adultery is wrong. In Romans 1, Paul strongly condemns the immoral lifestyle that characterized Roman and Greek society (Romans 1:18–32).

GOOD NEIGHBOURS (19: 1-37)

When Jesus is asked what is the greatest commandment, he replies: "Love the Lord your God with all your heart and with all your soul and with all your strength and with all your mind" and "Love your neighbour as yourself" (Luke 10:27). The second part of his answer comes from Leviticus 19 (verse 18). This command appears at the end of a section explaining what loving one's neighbour means for the people of Israel. God is teaching them that in all they do, in the way they live in the community, and in how they run their business, they are to consider not only what is good for themselves but also what will be good for their neighbours.

They are to care for those less fortunate than themselves and so, when reaping their harvest, they have to make sure they leave some grain and grapes to be gathered by those who are too poor to have their own fields: "When you harvest your fields, do not cut the corn at the edges of the fields, and do not go back to cut the ears of corn that were left. Do not go back through your vineyard to gather the grapes that were missed or to pick up the grapes that have fallen; leave them for poor people and foreigners" (19:9–10 GNB).

When Ruth and Naomi, her mother-in-law, move from Moab to live near Bethlehem, they are destitute and have no land of their own. Naomi encourages Ruth to go to a neighbour's field and gather the corn the reapers have left behind (Ruth 2:1–13). Ruth works in the fields of a man called Boaz, who is Naomi's distant relative. Boaz takes pity on this poor peasant girl, even though she is a foreigner, and allows her to work, not on the edges of the field but along with his reapers. He makes sure she is protected and is given water to drink. He subsequently offers to marry her, and their first child, Obed, becomes the grandfather of king David. It is a pleasant romantic story, but more important than that, it exemplifies one of the principles laid down in Leviticus, and illustrates the kind of generous and caring behaviour towards the poor and vulnerable God expects of his people.

The Old Testament Scriptures constantly speak of our responsibility to care for those who have less than we have (for example, Exodus 23:11). The prophets condemn the people of Israel for their constant abuse of the poor (Isaiah 3:14, Amos 2:7). Concern for the poor is a central feature of the ministry and teaching of Jesus (Matthew 19:21). Sadly, in today's secular and materialistic societies, it is too easy for the wealthy to want to get as much as possible for themselves and think little of others who lack sufficient food, proper housing or sanitation.

So, while millions die in affluent countries from obesity, more than seven million people die annually throughout the world because of hunger and malnutrition, according to statistics released by the United Nations in 2017. This means about twenty-one thousand people, on average, die every day through lack of food. This poses a challenge to those of us who claim to love God, for John asks us: "If anyone has material possessions and sees a brother or sister in need but has no pity on them, how can the love of God be in that person?" (1 John 3:17).

God's people are not only commanded to care for others. They are also told to be honest in their business dealings, to demonstrate integrity. They are not to deceive or defraud others but always to tell the truth. When they hear unkind rumours, they are not to pass them on and damage the reputation of others. They are not to do anything that may endanger someone else's life or cause them harm. If they find themselves in the position of a judge, they are to fulfil that role honestly and fairly, without prejudice or favour.

When they come across people who are blind or disabled, they are neither to take advantage of nor make fun of them. They must not exploit others but must always pay their employees a fair wage without delay. Many of the population in the time of the Old Testament were poor and depended on their daily wage. If it was withheld even for one or two nights, they and their family might suffer and have to go without food.

Being a just, fair and considerate employer is a mark of holiness. If God's people behave in this way, they are reflecting the character of the holy and merciful God whom they worshipped. Sadly, Christians, especially those in positions of leadership, have not always demonstrated these characteristics. When we do not follow the pattern set out in Leviticus 19:9–18, we negate any witness we may share verbally.

Respect the elderly and care for immigrants

Leviticus 19:32–34 emphasises the need to show respect for the elderly. It was recognised in the ancient world that the elderly had gained wisdom and experience which could be of value to the younger generations (verse 32). While respect for the elderly is retained in many cultures in the majority world, in the West it has been replaced by the giving of pride of place to the young. Isaiah points out that lack of respect for those who are older is one of the marks of the disintegration of a society (Isaiah 3:5).

God's people are also commanded to welcome immigrants and treat them fairly. They are told to love them (19:33–34). In 2020, some twenty-six million people were forced to flee their own countries, leaving familiar lands behind and becoming refugees. They had fled their countries because of persecution, war or violence. Over two-thirds of them come from just five countries: Syria, Afghanistan, South Sudan, Myanmar and Somalia. The natural human response is to ignore this problem and presume that it is up to someone else to help these people in their dire need. But God's people are called to demonstrate the love of God to those in need, just as God has shown his love to us in our need. Christians should be in the forefront of doing all they can to welcome refugees and helping them to find a new home.

CELEBRATIONS AND HOLIDAYS (23:1-44)

In Leviticus 23, the people of God are told to keep a number of special days and religious festivals. These occasions allow the people to remember all that God has done, and to offer him worship and praise. They also give the people time to rest. The Israelites are taught to observe a weekly day of rest and take at least three weeks' holiday a year. God believes in holidays, which is good news!

The Sabbath, observed weekly, is intended as a day of rest and the people are commanded not to do any work (verse 3). Rabbinic law lists thirty-nine examples of work that are forbidden on the Sabbath, and these include cooking food or lighting a fire. Sometimes it is difficult to know what is permitted and what is not. A Jewish mother, who was a friend of ours, asked her rabbi if her son was allowed to play cricket on the Sabbath day. The rabbi told her that her son could not because the hard ball might split the cricket bat, and that would be tantamount to cleaving wood, which was forbidden on the Sabbath. However, her son could play tennis because that was played with soft balls which would not crack the tennis racket. It may seem strange to make such fine distinctions about trivial details, but the attitude of the mother reflected the sincerity with which devout Jewish believers seek to obey God's law and observe this special day.

The Sabbath is also designated as a day for the worship of God: "It is a Sabbath to the Lord" (Leviticus 23:3). Today, a devout Jew will spend the Sabbath in the synagogue or at home studying the holy books. This gives the Sabbath day a unique atmosphere of stillness and peace, which is understood as a foreshadowing of the peace of heaven. The Sabbath is more honoured than any other festival in the Jewish calendar. The German theologian, Rabbi Leo Baeck, believed that it was the observance of the Sabbath which enabled the Jewish people to survive as a community during the worst times of their persecution. He said: "There is no Judaism without the Sabbath. Today, it is regarded as the crowning glory in the life of a Jew."

A number of other festivals and special holy days are described in Leviticus 23, including *Passover*, *Pentecost* and *Tabernacles*. In later Jewish history these became known as the three pilgrim festivals, because once the Temple was built all the males in Israel were encouraged to go up to Jerusalem to celebrate these festivals.

The first pilgrim festival, the feast of Passover (verses 4–7), celebrates the night when God sent his angel of death and delivered his people from slavery. This is the greatest event in their history, when they gained their freedom and began the journey to the Promised Land. They are commanded to celebrate and rejoice in the goodness of the Lord. They are told to have a party—God encourages celebration and parties—and to do no work for eight days. During those eight days they are to eat only unleavened bread, as a reminder that when they escaped from Egypt they had to leave in a hurry. There was not time to make bread with yeast and to wait for the dough to rise.

Today, Jewish people celebrate Passover in their home with a special meal, called a *seder*, at which they use a service book, called a *Haggadah*. This literally means "telling" because it retells the story of the escape of the Israelites from slavery in Egypt. Jesus celebrates the Passover with his disciples the night before he dies, and it is during that meal that he institutes a new meal to commemorate, not the exodus from Egypt, but his death on the cross.

Fifty days or seven weeks after Passover, the people of Israel are told to celebrate the second pilgrim festival, sometimes called the Festival of Weeks or Pentecost (verses 15–21). This festival reminds the people of their journey through the wilderness to Mount Sinai where God gave them the Ten Commandments. Today, on the Day of Pentecost, in synagogues all over the world, the congregation will stand as the Ten Commandments are read. They praise God for giving them his law, written on tablets of stone. Over a thousand years after the giving of the law, God sent his Holy Spirit on the Day of Pentecost so that his word could be written not on stone but on human hearts.

The third pilgrim festival that the people of Israel are commanded to observe is the feast of Tabernacles (verses 33–43). The people are told: "On the first day you are to take branches from luxuriant trees—from palms, willows and other leafy trees—and rejoice before the Lord your God for seven days" (verse 40). Following these instructions, Jews living in Israel today will build temporary shelters and live in them for a week as a way of remembering the temporary shelters in which their ancestors lived as they travelled for forty years in the desert (John 7:37). This practice is not so keenly followed in the UK because the climate is unreliable and it rains too often!

The three pilgrim festivals, together with other special days observed during the year, enable Jewish people to remember the various ways in which God has guided and blessed them. As Christians, we have even more reason to be grateful for the grace God has shown towards us. Many churches follow a set calendar or liturgical year in order to remember what God has done for believers in Christ. The church year starts with Advent when we remember the first coming of Jesus and look forward to his return. This is followed by the celebration of his birth. On Good Friday we remember his death on the cross, and on Easter Day we celebrate his resurrection. At the festival of Pentecost, we thank God for the gift of his Holy Spirit.

JUSTICE AND EQUALITY (25: 1-55)

Leviticus 25 is an amazing chapter setting out a vision for a just, compassionate and equal society. Many nations may aim for such an idyllic state but few, if any, ever achieve it. The people of God are called to reflect God's character not only in their personal spiritual and social life but also in the way they conduct their political life. This is the biblical pattern for an ideal society. Over the years, it has proved a source of inspiration and controversy among theologians, social reformers and politicians.

Every seventh year, the people of Israel are to leave their fields fallow (verses 1–7). They are not allowed to plough, sow, reap or harvest. They are to let the land have a rest, just as God had a rest on the seventh day in the creation story. The purpose of this agricultural sabbatical is to allow the resources of the earth to be replenished and stop the land becoming exhausted and infertile. The people have to trust that God will provide them with enough food to eat during this time.

Every fiftieth year is to be celebrated as a Year of Jubilee. All debts are to be cancelled and all lands restored to the original owners (verses 8–24). This will be necessary because, over the years, some families may have fallen into debt, forcing them to give up their land and property. Some rules are in place to help them in their time of need and enable them to try to repay their debts, but, inevitably, there will be those who are still heavily in debt after many years. Some may be forced to sell themselves and members of their family to become hired domestic servants.

In the Year of Jubilee, all remaining debts will be wiped out. Those who have become yoked to others as domestic servants will regain their freedom and return to their own property. The land is regarded as belonging to God and he is the one who has allotted a certain portion of the land to each family. The legislation for the Year of Jubilee makes it possible for every family to be restored to their land at least once in each generation. This will lead to a levelling out of society, enabling those who may get sucked further and further into debt to be saved from that terrible spiral, while preventing others from becoming ever richer and imposing their will on the rest of society.

God has demonstrated his concern for the environment and instructed his people not to over-farm the land. Now he is showing them that he is equally concerned with the rights of the homeless and the dangers of economic exploitation. Holiness is not simply a matter of personal piety. It has implications for the social and political life of a nation.

The small print (26: 1-46)

When you read any legal document, it is always important to read the small print. Some documents, drawn up by a lawyer or an insurance company, are lengthy and written in legal jargon, and it is not always easy to understand exactly what the document is saying. I remember taking out an insurance policy for our home which included cover for our valuable personal possessions, when outside the home. When a freak wind blew over my expensive telescope, I assumed it would be covered by the insurance policy. Butt was not. There was some exclusion in the legal minutiae I had failed to understand.

In reading through Leviticus, it is easy to miss the significance of some of the small print. This is particularly the case as so much of this book contains references to customs which appear strange and reflect a culture very different from our own. While many of the laws seem irrelevant to us, it is important that we take seriously the underlying message. This is the word of God given to his people, in which he commands them to be holy. More than any other book, Leviticus emphasises again and again that these laws are not human ideas but

God's word. Fifty-six times in these twenty-seven chapters, we read the words: "The Lord says." There is no doubt who the author is.

God calls his people to be holy and obedient and to reflect his character in every aspect of our lives—in the kind of people we are, in our family life, in our sexual life, in our neighbourly relations, in our behaviour at work, in our social life, in our help for those in need, in our involvement in the reform and improvement of society. God makes it abundantly clear that the way we behave can have serious consequences on others.

The penultimate chapter of Leviticus contains a stern warning to the people of God of what may happen if they persistently reject his love and disobey his commands: "But if you will not listen to me and carry out all these commands, and if you reject my decrees and abhor my laws and fail to carry out all my commands and so violate my covenant, then I will do this to you: I will bring on you sudden terror, wasting diseases and fever that will destroy your sight and sap your strength. You will plant seed in vain, because your enemies will eat it" (26:14–16).

These verses should give us some cause for concern, if we are constantly disobedient and flouting God's laws. But we can be comforted and encouraged by the corresponding verses that describe the blessings of material provision and divine protection and presence that will come to those who are obedient. God promises: "I will look on you with favour and make you fruitful and increase your numbers, and I will keep my covenant with you…I will put my dwelling place among you, and I will not abhor you. I will walk among you and be your God, and you will be my people" (26:9, 11–12).

LIVE A HOLY LIFE TODAY

Personal purity: Sexual entanglements are among the most challenging issues that confront Christians. In modern society, especially in the West, it is all too easy for us as Christians to conform to the moral standards of our secular and self-absorbed society, which assumes that each person can do whatever they feel is right for them. Paul warns us in Romans not to be conformed to this world but to be transformed by the renewing of our minds.

Many Christians struggle with the issue of homosexual practice, which is addressed in Leviticus (18:22). The biblical teaching given here and elsewhere emphasises the need for sexual purity and makes it clear that the only appropriate context for sexual relationships is within marriage. The scriptural ideal, set out in Genesis 2, is for marriage to be a life-long union between one man and one woman, with the purpose of providing mutual comfort and support, and for the procreation of children. Derek Tidball, former principal of London Bible College raises a critical question when he asks: "How far does contemporary research into the causes of homosexuality change the prohibition in Scripture?" (*Leviticus,* Crossway, p.149).

One of the problems faced by Western society is its obsession with sex and its elevation of physical intercourse as the ultimate expression of love. While we can rejoice in physical love as a marvellous gift from our creator, it is also true that many enjoy the deepest and closest friendship without any expression of their love in sexual terms. Jesus himself describes the greatest expression of love as the laying down of one's life for one's friends.

Community engagement: As a reflection of God's character it is our responsibility to do all we can to help those who are poor, disabled or vulnerable (19:8-10, 13-15). How far is our local church involved in care for the elderly, the lonely, the single parent family or those who are unemployed? How far are we even aware of the critical social needs in our community? Are we content just to carry on preaching the gospel in our churches and hoping people will attend? James calls for our faith to be shown in concrete acts of love, not just verbal expressions of what we believe.

When we were living in East Asia, we often noticed that Buddhists and Muslims came to faith not through reading a tract or hearing a sermon, but through Christians showing them love in practical ways. One Indonesian Christian got up early every day to take coffee to those working in the rice paddy fields. Eventually one of the farmers asked why she did this. She replied that she wanted to thank them for working hard so people like her would have rice to eat every day. She added that she also did it to show them how much God loved them. The farmer was so struck by her words that he invited her into his home to talk about the love of God. Others came to listen as she told them week after week about how God had shown his love to the world. In time several people in the community came to faith and were baptised.

Environmental action: Christians must take care of the world which God has given them as their home. They are not simply to take from the land everything they can possibly get. Every seventh year the Israelites are told not to cultivate their land but to allow it to remain fallow (25:1–7). They are also commanded to give newly planted fruit trees enough time to grow before they start harvesting their crop (19:23–25). Such teaching, together with the threat posed to our planet by climate change, challenges us to consider how we have overused the resources we have and how we need to re-examine our lifestyle.

The Year of Jubilee is a reminder to the people that the land does not belong to them but to God. They are merely tenants. God makes it clear that he wishes every family to have a fair share of the use of the land and families that have fallen into debt and lost their property can have a chance to regain their property. In our day there are many nations in the two-thirds world that struggle with ever-mounting debt to more developed countries. They have little prospect of escaping from that vicious cycle of poverty. Leviticus challenges rich Christians to see what they should do to alleviate this situation and how they can bring pressure on their governments to release nations from crippling debts.

God's people are called to be a holy people. That means more than attending a place of worship, walking around with a pious expression or quoting passages from the Bible. It means demonstrating the purity of God in our lives, the justice of God in our actions in our community, and the love of God in acts of kindness, compassion and generosity.

FOR PERSONAL REFLECTION

1. How far do we conform to the moral standards of the world in our sexual behaviour? What can help us to be transformed both in our actions and in our thought life?

2. In what practical ways is your church involved in care for the elderly, the unemployed, the disabled and immigrants? What more can you do?

3. What can Christians learn from the various Jewish festivals about celebrating God's goodness and remembering what he has done?

4. What are the ways in which God promises to bless his people (26:1-13)? Should we expect God to bless us materially? On what Scriptures would you base your answer?

Section 2

Community Transformation

How Do We Live with One Another?

Chapter 5

A Family of Faith

Some people who say they are Christians never go to church. Of course, it is true that you do not have to go to church to be a Christian, but it is equally true that you may well not survive as a Christian when you face serious problems in your life, if you do not have the fellowship and support of other believers. Scripture makes it clear that when you become a Christian, you become a member of God's family. Normally we expect members of the same family to talk to each other and do what they can to help one another. Paul reminds us that we should meet together regularly with other members of God's family. We should be concerned for them, encourage them and help them to grow as Christians.

In the opening chapters of the book of Numbers, God helps the people whom he has rescued from slavery in Egypt to prepare for their long journey through the desert. He reminds them that they belong together as one community. They are now the people of God, the family of God, but within that family each individual is important. That why this book begins, and ends, with a census. Every person is counted because every one is of significance to God. Yet these individuals do not exist in isolation from each other. They belong to one another. They face the trials of their journey together. They worship God, celebrate his goodness and experience his blessings together.

Numbers 1–10

In Genesis, God makes a covenant with Abraham and his descendants and promises to make them a great nation, to give them a land, and to make them a blessing to the world. In Exodus, he delivers Abraham's descendants from slavery in Egypt, adopts them as his people, gives them his law, and comes to live among them in the Tabernacle. In Leviticus, he shows the people how they are to dwell in his presence, how they are to draw near to him in worship, and how they are to live as his holy people. In Numbers, he prepares them for their journey to the land promised to their ancestor Abraham, a journey that should have taken ten days but takes forty years.

The book of Numbers is essentially a diary. It is Moses' personal record of the journey that he and the people of Israel take for four decades through the desert. Although we know this book as Numbers, its title in Hebrew is "In the Desert" (1:1), which seems an appropriate title for a diary written about a trek through the wilderness. In this diary, at God's command, "Moses recorded the stages in their journey" (33:2), and kept an account of the places the people passed through.

The first ten chapters of Numbers deal with the preparations made for the long march. The middle section (11–20) records a number of significant events that occur as the people wander through the desert. We see how often they fail to trust God and how frequently they complain to Moses and criticise him. Moses, for his part, learns some hard lessons about being a spiritual leader, eventually becoming very angry with the people. The final section of the book (21–36) covers the period when the Israelites are approaching their ultimate destination. We learn of the opposition and hostility they face, the battles they have to fight, and the plans that are made for the invasion and settlement of the Promised Land.

Moses keeps this diary to remind the people of their long and arduous journey, and to encourage them not to repeat their mistakes. He wants them to remember how God is constantly blessing, leading and protecting them. He also wants them to see what a privilege it is for them to belong to the family of God, and in the first ten chapters he details God's blessings over each of them.

THE FAMILY WHERE EVERYONE COUNTS (1: 1 – 2:34)

At the beginning of the book, slightly over a year after the Israelites have come out of Egypt, God commands Moses to take a census of the people. At the end of the book, almost forty years later, he is told to repeat the exercise. The fact that the people are counted twice resulted in the book being given the title "Numbers." Moses is told to record the names of all the men who are able to serve in the army "listing every man by name, one by one" (1:2). Here is a full list of those over the age of twenty and able to fight. The numbers are huge. The fighting force numbers over six hundred thousand. If you add women, children and the elderly, this implies a community of between two and three million. This is about the same as the population of Egypt at the time and ten times the population of Canaan.

The problem with these large numbers is that they are out of proportion with the numbers of people in the region at the time. Some scholars have pointed out that in the original Hebrew text, which was written without the vowels, there are two words that appear to be identical. One word means one thousand, while the other means a leader or captain. It is certainly possible that in the course of copying the text over the centuries the word for captain had been translated as one thousand men. So, for example, a tribe that had forty-five leaders or officers and five hundred men could have been translated as having forty-five thousand and five hundred. We cannot be sure that this is what happened but it is plausible. While there is some degree of uncertainty as to how we should understand the numbers, it is clear that the community of Israelites is huge.

69

The detailed census in Numbers 1 lists every soldier who is able to fight in the army. While only the men are counted, the census is regarded as a registration of the whole community. Every man, woman and child is involved in this epic journey through the wilderness to the Promised Land. The men who are counted represent individual family units. While the immediate purpose of the exercise is to assess the strength of the army, it also provides a census of the whole community.

The survey is carried out in a systematic and orderly way. Moses appoints one man from each tribe to organise the census within their tribe, dividing them into clans, kin groups and families. Each person's name is recorded, because all have their place within the tribal division in the army. As a modern army may be divided into regiments, battalions and platoons, so the army of the Israelites is divided into tribes, clans and smaller units. Each individual is counted because each is important, as we have noted, but they all belong to the same army and serve the same Lord. Each plays his part in battle, fighting alongside and depending on the soldier fighting next to him.

Firstly, here is a picture of the people of God as one body made up of individuals, all of whom are mutually dependent on each other. This picture is frequently developed in the New Testament as a description of the church (Romans 12:4–8, 1 Corinthians 12:1–31, Ephesians 4:16). The people of God belong to one body. They are on a pilgrimage together and they struggle side by side in mutual support. Such an understanding of the people of God contradicts any idea that an individual believer should try to live in isolation. No one should say that he or she believes in God but wants nothing to do with members of God's family. We all discover that other believers are not perfect (unlike ourselves!) and that some of them have irritating manners, but that is no reason to refuse to work, worship, or have fellowship with them.

Secondly, we see that everyone, who is the right age, is enlisted for service. Doubtless some of the young men are strong and broad-shouldered, while others are less muscular. But they are all enlisted. A quick overview of the biblical story will reinforce the point that, while God does use some exceptionally gifted people, most of those he calls to a specific task have flaws and demonstrate significant areas of weakness. Paul spells out to the Christians at Corinth that there was nothing exceptional about them. They were neither rich nor aristocratic; they were neither particularly gifted nor attractive, yet God chose them and brought them into his family (1 Corinthians 1:26–29).

In any local church it is not uncommon for members to compare themselves unfavourably to others in the congregation, who appear to be far more gifted or more spiritual than they are. They can easily convince themselves they are second-class Christians, who can never play a significant role in the church. Yet the picture provided in Numbers 1 is of the people of God as a community in which everyone is important.

Thirdly, we see a picture of the people of God being called to serve in the army of their King, ready to fight alongside one another against any who would attack them. Jesus tells his disciples that they will be engaged in a spiritual war. Peter says: "Be alert and of sober mind. Your enemy the devil prowls around like a roaring lion, looking for someone to devour" (1 Peter 5:8). But whereas in the book of Numbers, only men aged twenty and over are drafted into the fighting force, in the New Testament all God's people, irrespective of age or gender, are called to serve the Lord Jesus and to fight as a good solider of Christ Jesus, who seeks only to please his commanding officer (2 Timothy 2:3–4).

In spite of their weakness and sinfulness, God's people will not be defeated but will complete the task to which they are called. If we compare the census at the beginning of Numbers and that at the end, we will see that the numbers remain about the same. Some clans have shrunk, others have grown but the overall number is virtually constant. In spite of the people's mistakes, their constant grumbling, their criticism of Moses, their rebellion and lack of faith, they continue their journey to the Promised Land.

As we look around at the church in the UK and elsewhere in the West, we witness a decline in church attendance and the marginalisation of Christian influence in society, and we may be tempted to despair. But when we look around the world to Asia, Africa and Latin America, we see that in many countries the church has experienced rapid growth. The book of Numbers illustrates that God always perseveres with his people. When Peter declares that Jesus is the Messiah, the Son of the living God, Jesus replies: "And I tell you that you are Peter, and on this rock I will build my church, and the gates of Hades will not overcome it" (Matthew 16:18). Jesus assures Peter that all the forces of evil and destruction (the gates of hell) will not be able to prevail against the people of God.

THE FAMILY WHICH IS LED IN WORSHIP (3:1 – 6:21)

The Tabernacle is set up in the middle of the Israelite camp and the twelve tribes are arranged in a square around God's tent, with three tribes on each point of the compass. When Alexander the Great led his armies, his tent lay in the middle of the army camp and was marked by a tall spear, so everyone knew that he was in their midst. Likewise, the people of Israel know that their God is living among them, which brings them confidence in their future victory.

Immediately next to the Tabernacle are the tents of the Levites. It is the job of the priests and the Levites to look after the Tabernacle, maintaining it so that it is fit for the worship of God. These priests and Levites are listed in Number 3–4. First, there is the High Priest, the only one who can go into the presence of God in the Holy of Holies. He is assisted in his religious duties by other priests, originally the four sons of Aaron.

Then there are the Levites, consisting of all the other descendants of Levi and his three sons—Gershon, Kohath and Merari. They are responsible for the upkeep and purity of the Tabernacle. Each clan has specific duties and has to look after a particular part of the Tabernacle. The Levites are also responsible for the transportation of the Tabernacle. They have to take it down when the people break camp and move on in their journey, and reassemble it at the next camp. Everything has to be done correctly and in a precise order. They have to be very careful to show due reverence, for they are dealing with holy things: "But they must not touch the holy things or they will die" (4:15). Only the priests are allowed to look at or touch the unveiled holy things.

The priests, assisted by the Levites, are also responsible for maintaining the ritual and physical cleanliness in the camp, and for exercising discipline in the community. They are to handle cases of cheating, slander or marital unfaithfulness. One case is cited where a man suspects his wife has been flirting with another man and may even be pregnant with another man's child. It is the job of the priests to ascertain if the accusation is true.

While the priests and the Levites are appointed by God to serve in the Tabernacle, there are some Israelite men and women who voluntarily dedicate themselves to God in an act of self-denial and commitment. They are told to take a vow of dedication to God, usually for a limited period. The men and women who dedicate themselves to God must faithfully observe what they promise. They have to avoid anything that would contaminate them. They are required to abstain from drinking alcohol and, as a mark of their period of dedication they must also refrain from cutting their hair. Those who undertake such a vow are called the Nazirites. If they become contaminated, for example, by touching a dead body, they will need to shave their head and offer sacrifices. It seems likely that both Samson and Samuel were Nazirites.

In some Christian traditions, men and women have undertaken vows of celibacy as they seek to serve God and devote themselves to prayer and service. In one sense all Christians make vows to God when they turn to Christ or make a renewed commitment to him. Across the world, Methodists at the beginning of a new year hold an annual covenant service, at which they celebrate all that God has done for them, and affirm their dedication to God. Whatever our personal church affiliation, it is salutary to reflect on the promises we have made to God and learn from the Nazirites the importance of being faithful to them. We may not feel called to become a pastor to serve in mission or development work overseas, but we are all called to serve God. We all have our roles to play in prayer, witness and service for the kingdom of God.

THE FAMILY WHICH IS BLESSED BY GOD (6:22–27)

The closing paragraph of Numbers 6 contains some of the most well-known words in the Old Testament. They are pronounced every Sabbath Day in the synagogue and are often used at the end of Christian services or celebrations. Aaron and his fellow priests are told to pronounce this blessing over the people of Israel: "The Lord bless you and keep you; the Lord make his face shine on you and be gracious to you; the Lord turn his face toward you and give you peace" (6:24–26).

What does it mean to bless someone? Why do people say, "bless you" when they hear someone sneeze? Why do some respond to an act of kindness by saying, "bless you"? Sometimes these two words may have little significance other than being an expression of goodwill. However, in the case of the Aaronic blessing, the words carry great meaning.

In the Bible the significance of pronouncing a blessing can be illustrated by the blessing given by a dying father to his children. Isaac blesses his two sons (Genesis 27:26ff). Jacob blesses each of his twelve sons (Genesis 49). Those blessings spoken out loud have the same legal force as a written will. Once blessings have been pronounced, they cannot be revoked. In the story of creation, God blesses all that he has made. That blessing carries with it the guarantee that everything on the earth would grow and be fruitful. When the priests declare God's blessing, they are giving a blessing not from themselves but from God.

The blessing given by Aaron promises God's protection: "The Lord bless you and keep you" (6:24). It speaks of God making his face shine on those who are blessed. When the sun shines on us we feel its warmth. When people smile at us, we feel their love. When God's face shines on us, we know that he loves us and, in his grace, accepts us as we are. When he turns his face towards us, we know that he is not looking at us as a judge who might pronounce condemnation but as a loving father who welcomes us as his beloved children.

THE FAMILY WHICH GIVES GENEROUSLY (7:1 – 8:26)

When Rosemary and I were living in Singapore, the church we attended, St John's–St Margaret's (SJSM), grew in numbers until the original sanctuary was no longer adequate for the needs of the congregation. The church decided to redevelop the site and build a much larger place for worship. The cost was enormous, running into millions of dollars. I wondered how such a large sum could be raised, but God moved his people to give. When the building was completed all the costs had been covered. Paul tells the church in Corinth that God loves a cheerful giver (2 Corinthians 9:7), and I felt that was exactly what the congregation of SJSM demonstrated in their generosity.

This generosity is evident is Numbers 7 as the leaders of each of the twelve tribes bring huge gifts to pay for the cost of their sanctuary, the Tabernacle. This chapter, the longest in the Bible apart from Psalm 119, records the magnificent gifts that are presented by the representatives of each tribe for the furnishings of the Tabernacle, their transportation and the maintenance of its services. Six wagons, each pulled by two oxen, are needed to convey the Tabernacle and all its furniture from place to place. The responsibility for the provision of these wagons is shared between the twelve tribes. Each tribe is also required to provide a silver bowl, a silver basin filled with shekels of gold, and a ladle filled with incense, as well as a number of bulls, rams, lambs and goats that will be offered in sacrifice.

The gifts are presented in a splendid and lengthy ceremony. Whether a particular tribe is large and important in the hierarchy of the tribes, such as Judah, or small and insignificant, such as Naphtali, they are all recognised in the same way and enjoy the same prominence in the procession. All the tribes are called to participate in the worship of God, in whose presence all men and women are equal. As Paul reminds us: "There is neither Jew nor Gentile, neither slave nor free, nor is there male and female, for you are all one in Christ Jesus (Galatians 3:28). It is not the wealth of any individual or tribe that is important. Each gift is a token of appreciation to God and is of equal importance to him. In the story of the poor widow who only gives two tiny coins to the upkeep of the Temple, Jesus declares that she has given more than all the rich people, because she has given all that she has (Luke 21:1–4).

It takes twelve days for each of the tribes to make their presentations to the Tabernacle. Once everything has been offered, the seven-branch golden candlestick which stands at the front of the sanctuary is lit for the first time (8:1–4). The Levites are then ceremonially ordained. Everything is now set and the people are ready to begin their journey to the Promised Land. It only remains for last-minute preparations to be made and they can at last leave Mount Sinai where they have been camped for almost two years.

THE FAMILY WHICH IS FULL OF JOY (9:1–14)

Before starting out on their journey, the people are commanded to celebrate the Passover (Numbers 9). The first Passover has been celebrated in Egypt. Now, living as a free nation near Mount Sinai, the people can look back and remember that great act of God in delivering them from slavery. They are only free and able to go to the Promised Land because lambs died in Egypt on that terrible night when the people were spared from the angel of death.

For three thousand years the Jewish people have celebrated the Passover. It is the most joyful of all their religious festivals, marked by the wearing of new clothes and eating special food. It is a time to get together with family and friends to remember God's grace and goodness towards them.

God loves to see his people celebrating. In the gospels, Jesus is often recorded as being present at dinner parties and great banquets. So much so that he is criticised by some religious leaders for being too much of a partygoer. They complain he does not encourage his disciples to fast and spend too much time eating and drinking with people of dubious character (Luke 5:27–32). On the night of his death, Jesus celebrates the Passover with his disciples and looks forward to the time when they would celebrate together in the kingdom of heaven.

Joy is one of the fruits of the Spirit (Galatians 5:22). Jesus wishes that his disciples will be full of joy (John 15:11, 16:22). Yet Christians do not always give the impression that they are joyful people. Sometimes we can appear to be long-faced and serious. I remember talking to a Jewish taxi driver who had attended one or two services in a church. "It was so boring," he said. "There was nothing like the sense of joy we have in our synagogue." I have met Christians who have left their church because the services were so sombre and joyless. Of course, Christians are not meant to go around with a permanent grin on their faces. That could be artificial and unreal. But Christians should demonstrate that they have an inner peace and joy which the world cannot take away. A Muslim in Pakistan remarked: "If Christians talk about being saved, they should look more saved!"

THE FAMILY WHERE GOD IS THE HEAD (9:15–10:36)

Some families have a plaque in their home which reads: "Christ is the head of the home, the unseen guest at every meal, the silent listener to every conversation." The people of Israel know that God is living among them, as he has promised to dwell among them in the Tabernacle. They have seen the glory of God—which has appeared on the top of Mount Sinai—come down and enter the centre of the sanctuary. What a privilege to have God living among them. What a responsibility! It means the people are constantly aware that God is the head of the family. He is present at every meal. He hears every conversation.

After celebrating the Passover, the Israelites are ready to start their journey and God is going to go with them. His presence is indicated by a pillar of cloud by day and a pillar of fire by night. When the cloud moves forward, the people are to follow. God is with them both as guide and protector. With assurance of God's presence and direction given by a series of trumpet calls, the whole company begin their epic journey.

In every home where there is a believer, Jesus is present. In every Christian family, he is the head. How often we ignore that truth and behave as if he lives a thousand miles away. How easily we forget that he hears every word and knows our every thought. How often we worry ourselves sick about what we should do in a crisis and forget his promise to be with us: "And surely I am with you always, to the very end of the age" (Matthew 28:20). When we need guidance, he is the one who will guide our steps, just as he guided the people of Israel on their hazardous journey through the wilderness.

FOR PERSONAL REFLECTION

1. How important is it to you that you are a member of God's family? How much do you appreciate your brothers and sisters in Christ who belong to your local church? To what extent do you view them as fellow pilgrims and do what you can to help them on their spiritual journey?

2. The words "As the Lord commanded" appear throughout the whole of Numbers (1:19, 54; 2:34; 3:16, 42, 51, etc). Why is this phrase repeated so often and what does it tell us about our spiritual journey?

3. There is a strong emphasis on purity in Numbers 5–6, and in the whole of the Bible (1 Corinthians 6:18–20, Ephesians 5:5). What does God expect of us? How do you cope with temptations that come to you through the media, the Internet, or your social life?

4. Each of the tribes makes extravagant gifts for the cost of the furnishings of the Tabernacle. In 2 Corinthians 9:6–9, Paul exhorts Christians to give generously towards the work of God and the needs of others. What practical advice and encouragement do you find in Paul's words?

Chapter 6

A Leader in Crisis

Many of us are very busy people. We are not able to fit into our day everything that we want to do and are unrealistic about what we can achieve in the space of twenty-four hours. Some people are particularly prone to take on more and more and have cope with increasing responsibilities. When they feel exhausted, they wonder if they can keep going. This can be true of any one of us and it certainly includes those engaged in Christian ministry. Some assume, mistakenly, that they must be available to help others every moment of the day and night. They are committed to their work and are so conscientious that they try to do everything they possibly can themselves rather than trouble others. This is the danger facing Moses as he leads the children of Israel through the wilderness. In Numbers 11, we see how he reaches the point of exhaustion and despair. He has to learn to face his own limitations and understand his need to share the burden of leadership with others.

Another pressure Moses faces is criticism. He is criticised when he first goes to Egypt to rescue the Israelites and he is criticised when they leave Mount Sinai to begin their epic journey to the Promised Land. But the most painful experience of criticism he faces is recorded in Numbers 12 when his own brother and sister attack him and his wife. His refusal to retaliate and his willingness to pray for them is a remarkable example of how to respond to criticism.

Numbers 11–12

The people of Israel have spent two glorious years on Sinai. God has adopted them as his people. He has given them his law and shown them how they can draw near to him in worship. As they set out for the Promised Land they are full of faith and optimism. In a matter of weeks, they will be able to enter the inheritance that God promised to their ancestors, a land flowing with milk and honey.

You may expect that they would be a very grateful people after their amazing rescue from Egypt and their dramatic encounter with God on the mountain, and now with their new life in the Promised Land in sight. Sadly, they do not seem to appreciate all that God has done for them at all and within three days (10:33) they start to grumble (11:4–6). They complain about the hardships they have experienced. They seem to have forgotten what life was like in Egypt when they were treated badly, forcibly conscripted to build cities for Pharaoh. They have forgotten that they were often beaten by their taskmasters and their baby boys were drowned in the river Nile.

How like us they are! How quickly we also forget what God has done for us and how much he has blessed us. How often we fail to express our appreciation and gratitude to him. How easily we focus our attention on the problems of daily life. How often we concentrate on what we have not been given rather than being grateful for all that we have.

In particular, the people complain about the food. They long for a decent steak and have a craving for the fresh fruit and vegetables they enjoyed in Egypt—cucumbers, melons, leeks, onions and garlic. We have no idea how often they were able to eat food like that when they were working as Pharaoh's slaves. When Rosemary and I were living in rural Ethiopia, people had little access to fresh vegetables and would only rarely be able to afford meat. But it is easy to let one's imagination get carried away and to create a totally unrealistic picture of "the good old days."

The Israelites have been feeding on the manna God miraculously provided for them in the wilderness, but they are now fed up with it.

They have tried every recipe for serving it up in different ways but they are bored with it and long for something else. They do not just complain; they moan and groan (11:2, 4). s the wailing of the people and do not know what to do. This huge crowd of people are clamouring at the door of his tent, expecting him to sort out the crisis.

The pressures piled on Moses provide powerful lessons for anyone who aspires to exercise leadership among God's people. More pages of the Scriptures are devoted to describing the life and ministry of Moses than to anyone else apart from the Lord Jesus. It is good for leaders, whether of a small fellowship or a mega-church, to consider the challenges Moses faces and the way in which, through God's grace, he responds to them.

THE PRESSURE OF OVERWORK (11:1-35)

When Moses hears the crowd complaining at the entrance to his tent, his reaction is to say: "I cannot cope with this. I cannot possibly produce meat for all these people. I do not know why God has given me this job. It is not as if they are my family. I have two sons and maybe I can provide for them, but I certainly cannot cope with tens of thousands. This is just an impossible situation. If this is what it means to be the leader of Israel, forget it. I would rather die!" (See 11:10–15.)

Moses was in a similar situation some years before. When his father-in-law, Jethro, came to visit him near Mount Sinai, he discovered that Moses was wearing himself out by trying to resolve every dispute and petty conflict that arose in the camp. Jethro pointed out that he could not possibly carry on like that and advised him to share his work with others. If Moses delegated responsibility for the minor cases, he could concentrate on the more serious ones.

Moses was reluctant to do this because he felt it was part of his job description. After all, he was the one who had been prepared for this task. He had received a high education (Acts 7:22). He had grown up in the seat of government. He had been called dramatically by God to be the leader and deliverer of his people. But he was persuaded to follow his father-in-law's advice. He carefully selected capable and trustworthy men, trained them and gave them areas of responsibility according to their ability. So far, so good.

But now, two years later, Moses faces a similar dilemma. It appears he has not learned his lesson. He is again overwhelmed by the burden of leadership. He is convinced he must carry the nation on his shoulders and it is proving too much. He cannot cope any more and he feels like giving up (11:14). He has no idea that being the leader of God's people would be so demanding.

Moses is a conscientious man. He sees himself as being indispensable and the fount of all wisdom. The problem is that to an extent he is right. He does know more than others; he does know the Lord more intimately than anyone else; and he is more gifted. However, he is driving himself to an early grave—well, a relatively early grave as he has already turned eighty.

God's advice is not dissimilar to that given by Jethro: Share the responsibility. God says: "Delegate your authority to others. Let them share the burden of leadership. Choose seventy men who are recognised as leaders either by their age, status within the community or ability. Bring them to the tent of meeting and I will fill them with my Spirit and they will carry the burden with you." (See 11:16–17.)

One of the hardest lessons for Christian leaders to learn is the importance of delegating responsibility to others, training them and then trusting them to carry out their tasks. As leaders, we can easily assume we are indispensable and that everything depends on us. We think we have to make all the decisions and carry the heat of the day. In one church, the choir were not allowed to pray unless the vicar was with them. In another, a couple had developed a thriving ministry among young married couples, but the pastor put a stop to it, insisting that only he could run this significant ministry. In yet another church, the vicar closed down the missionary committee because he did not want others to make decisions without his approval.

It is easy for leaders to overestimate their gifts and to underestimate the competence and spiritual maturity of others. When I attended a Lausanne conference in Thailand in 1989, I met a bishop from a major denomination in southern Africa. He explained to me that their annual conference had to be chaired by a presiding bishop from the West, because "clearly we Africans are thought to be incapable of chairing such a meeting!"

The New Testament lays great emphasis on the fact that God endows each member of the body of Christ with different gifts, which they are to exercise for the benefit of the whole body (Ephesians 4:11–13). Paul says that the task of pastors, teachers and evangelists is to equip every member of their congregation so they can exercise their ministry. There are to be no passengers in Christ's church. Each has an important role to fulfil.

The pastor of a large church in Bangkok told me that he used to make all the decisions in his church and carry out all the functions of ministry and leadership. He did not allow anyone else to exercise his or her gifts. One day, as he was praying, he heard God say: "Let my people go!" So, he started to encourage members of the church to develop their gifts of ministry and to share in the decision-making process, with the result that they grew in maturity and the church experienced exponential growth.

When leaders fail to rest

If we are in leadership, whether as a senior pastor of a large congregation or a youth worker in a small church, we need to ask if we are suffering from fatigue. Do we feel, as Moses feels, that we are at the end of our tether, that we are almost too tired to go on? Do we find we are in a vicious circle where we just cannot stop working, because if we try to stop, we will just fall apart? I remember one pastor who told me that he felt he was on treadmill, that although he was exhausted, he could not stop but had to carry on. He was sure that if he got off the treadmill, he would have a breakdown.

If we feel like this, or if we know someone struggling in this way, we need to help them look at their workload. What are they doing that they do not need to do? What are they doing that they can easily delegate to others? This is such an important lesson for us to learn. The fact is that the demands and expectations put on ministers of the gospel are excessive and at times intolerable. It is small wonder that so many pastors and Christian workers collapse under the pressure.

One Japanese missionary was told by his pastor never to take a day of rest because, on the basis of Hebrews 4, the pastor argued that our Sabbath rest is in heaven. Another missionary was so dedicated to her work that she refused to take a holiday and was unwilling to let her colleague have a break either. When I was ordained, my vicar told me how he had suffered a breakdown because he never took time off. He said it took him years to get over that breakdown. He insisted that I, as his curate, take plenty of time to rest. "If you rest well, you can work well," he said.

To avoid burnout, we need to recognise our limitations. We are not supermen or superwomen. We may be able to work under pressure for a short while, but if we keep on pushing ourselves and burning the candle at both ends, we will quickly burn out. A couple who worked in a Bible college dedicated themselves to helping the students. The wife was always having students round and listening to their problems. The more she cared, the more they came, but she reached a point of exhaustion. Her counsellor said she must learn to set boundaries.

There can be consequences for our family. Some men decide to marry but then act as if they were still single. They spend all their time at the office or working on their computer at home. I have seen wives abandon their Christian faith because their husbands are never around, and though they may preach the gospel of love they do not show love to their families. I have met the children of well-known Christian leaders who have turned away from Christ because, in the words of one: "My father never had time for me, so I do not have any time for my father's God."

When leaders feel threatened

The appointing of the seventy elders (11:24–25) solves one problem but creates another. All but two of the seventy gather with Moses in the Tent of Meeting and are filled with the Spirit. But two stay in the camp. They also receive the Spirit and begin to prophesy on their own. Joshua, Moses' young adjutant, is very concerned: "This is out or order. This is not how it should be. This is outside your control, Moses, and a threat to your authority. We cannot have every Tom, Dick or Medad doing their own thing" (11:28).

It is easy to feel threatened when others show initiative. Delegation brings risks. If you delegate responsibility to others, you may discover that they are better at doing some things than you are. They may be better teachers, better administrators, better at personal evangelism or better counsellors. The temptation can be for us to clamp down on their work. However, in so doing, we may discourage initiative and deprive the church of the blessing others can bring.

When Joshua goes running to Moses and asks him to rebuke the two men in question, Moses does not react in the way Joshua expects. He does not rebuke the men but appears to affirm their ministry. He discerns that these men have been filled with God's Spirit and he expresses his hope that more of God's people would exercise spiritual gifts, not fewer. Moses knows, as Paul would write centuries later, that it is important to test the spirits, but he discerns that what has happened is from God.

The way we react to the gifts and ministry of others reveals a lot about our motivation. If our prime motive is for our own glory and reputation, we may feel threatened and may try to prevent or discredit the ministry of others. If our primary concern is for the glory of God and the growth of his kingdom, we will rejoice as we discern that God is at work.

In one town in the United Kingdom there was an old church that was not being used and was in danger of being closed down. A group of evangelicals offered to use the church and raise the money needed to restore the building. While the vicar and parochial church council of the parish came to an agreement, diocesan authorities refused to give their permission and seemed to prefer the building to be closed down rather than be used for a new congregation. They were threatened by this new initiative.

It is better to rejoice in rather than be threatened by the gifts of others. When I led a small mission team in London, one of the members of the team had amazing creative gifts. She developed some wonderful all-age service formats that our team could use when we visited different churches. She did all the work and had the creative gifts, while I got much of the credit as team leader!

THE PRESSURE OF CRITICISM (12:1-16)

Another pressure Moses faces is that of criticism. This is his experience from his very first day back in Egypt. He is constantly criticised and misunderstood. His motives are called into question, as is his competence. If you read through the books of Exodus and Numbers you will find twelve separate occasions when Moses faced criticism. George Verwer, the founder of Operation Mobilization, warns: "If you are in leadership and expect not to be criticised, you are living on another planet."

In Numbers 12, Miriam and Aaron speak against Moses and his leadership. It is particularly painful that those who criticise him are the ones dearest and nearest to him. Miriam is the sister who held him as a baby, put him into the papyrus basket, pushed him into the river, watched him float along the Nile, spoke to the princess and arranged for their mother to look after her own son. She is also a worship leader who is filled with the Spirit and leads the sacred dance team (Exodus 15:20–21). Aaron is Moses' older brother, his companion and colleague. He has been with Moses from the beginning of their ministry. He is Moses' right-hand man and spokesman (Exodus 7:1–2). He is now the High Priest in Israel, the most important person in the community after Moses.

Miriam and Aaron are the closest members of Moses' team. Together they have seen the Lord guiding, providing for and protecting them. Now they have turned against Moses. How hard it is when your own family turn against you, when your own leadership team turns its back on you, when your closest spiritual colleagues stab you in the back.

What is worse is that Miriam and Aaron do not just attack Moses. They attack his family, his wife (12:1). It is one thing to be criticised yourself but it is much harder to bear when a member of your family is criticised. Zipporah, Moses' wife, is from Midian. She is foreign and clearly Miriam does not like her or the position she enjoys and the influence she has in Israel. Perhaps Miriam feels that her sister-in-law is an outsider rather than a member of the people of God.

Not only do Miriam and Aaron criticise Moses' family, but they also attack his unique role and ministry: "Hasn't God also spoken through us?" (Numbers 12:1–2). Perhaps this is the result of the time when the Spirit fell on the seventy elders. Aaron and Miriam may well have been included among them. In fact, Miriam is called a prophetess. Since they have received the Spirit, they say they have equal authority too. Their mistake is not that they claim to have spiritual gifts but that they challenge Moses' unique leadership position.

Criticism is a constant companion of leadership. It happens in the secular world. It happens in the church. Christians are often the worse critics. We can spiritualise our criticism. Take what happened at a church prayer meeting; someone who wanted the pastor to leave claimed to have received a word of prophecy in which the Lord said he wanted someone in leadership to go.

How to respond to personal criticism

Firstly, we should not be surprised if we are criticised. It may mean that we are doing exactly what God wants us to do. We will be criticised for things that we do and for things that we do not. As someone said to me when I became General Director of OMF International, we need to develop the skin of a rhinoceros.

Secondly, we should not take criticism personally. We need to listen to people, be sensitive to their feeling and recognise that they may be hurting. If we can understand their pain and ask why they are upset, it may help us to be more sympathetic in our response. It is good to try to analyse the reason for their criticism. They may well have a valid point even if they do not express themselves well and may overstate their case. It is also good to bear in mind that those who are criticising you may not be struggling against you but against the Lord.

Thirdly, we should not try to justify our actions when we are criticised. Moses is silent and leaves things to God. The biblical text says that he is the meekest man in all the earth (12:3). I presume Moses did not write those words, or was so humble he did not feel proud about writing it. There is a time, however, when it may be appropriate to explain a particular course of action. In 2 Corinthians Paul responds to the accusation that he keeps changing his mind and is unreliable (2 Corinthians 1:12–24). Later on, in the same letter, he answers the charge, being made by false teachers, that he is weak and not really an apostle at all (2 Corinthians 10–12).

Finally, we should pray for those who criticise us and ask the Lord to bring good out of the situation. Moses is asked to pray his critics. Miriam is struck by a serious skin disease which lasts for a week. Aaron is not punished in this way because he would then have been debarred forever from continuing in the office of High Priest. It is hard to pray for those who hurt or attack us; it is easier to respond in kind or to harbour resentment. May God help us to respond in a gracious and appropriate way.

FOR PERSONAL REFLECTION

1. Read 1 Corinthians 10:1–13. Paul says that the journey of the children of Israel through the wilderness is recorded in Scripture for our benefit. What lessons can we learn from their experience?

2. The people of Israel had been blessed in so many ways and yet as soon as they set out on their journey to the Promised Land they began to grumble. What causes complaints or division in your church? What do we grumble about? What will help us to be more content?

3. What do you find is the best way to respond to criticism?

4. Reflect on pressures you face in your work or ministry. Share them within your group and pray for each other.

Chapter 7

A Leader Faces Failure

When we are young, many of us have grand but often unrealistic ambitions about what we will like to do when we grow up. At the age of seven, I told my family that I wanted to be the Archbishop of Canterbury! When we become adults, we may have more modest hopes for what we can achieve and we may work hard to reach the goals we set ourselves. By the time we retire we will have realised our limitations and recognise that we cannot achieve all our hopes and dreams.

Moses' great ambition is to lead his people out of slavery and into the Promised Land where they can become a proud and independent nation. During his long life, he manages to fulfil much of his dream. When the Israelites first arrive on the very edge of the Promised Land, however, the people refuse to enter it, and Moses dream is shattered.

Many years later, when the Israelites again reach a point close to the Land, Moses makes what is perhaps the greatest mistake of his life. His patience with the people who are constantly complaining and criticising him eventually runs out and he loses his temper with them. In a moment of anger, he fails to obey God and, in consequence, is told that he will not be allowed to enter the land of Canaan with his people. It may be surprising for us to read that such a great man of God should face disappointments and moments of failure. Nonetheless, this should encourage us to know that when we do not achieve all we hope for, we are not the only ones!

Numbers 13–20

Within a few days of leaving Mount Sinai, the people start to complain. As their leader Moses faces immense challenges. We have seen in the previous chapter how he has to cope with the weight of his responsibilities and the pressure of being so exhausted that he feels like giving up. Not only that he also has to put up with a constant barrage of criticism levelled against him. Now, as the people continue on their journey through the desert, he faces even greater challenges to his leadership and tougher tests in his personal life.

THE INEVITABILITY OF DISAPPOINTMENT (13:1 – 14:45)

In Numbers 13–14 spies are sent to explore Canaan. This marks a turning point in the story of the exodus—a watershed in the history of Israel. It is the moment when the people who have come out of Egypt get as far as they are going to get. They make the fateful decision not to go in to the Promised Land, and are condemned for the next forty years to wander in the wilderness.

For Moses this turn of events is deeply disappointing. His dream is shattered, his vision rejected, his goal thwarted. It is likely that he has the dream of entering the Promised Land from childhood. Raised by his mother, he would have heard the stories of the patriarchs. He knew God had said to Abraham: "To you and your descendants I will give this land." He understood that Abraham's descendants would live in a foreign land for a long time, but one day God would bring them back to the land promised to Abraham.

As Moses grew up, he witnessed the brutality his people suffered and he longed to do something to help. As a young man, he sought to intervene on their behalf. The book of Hebrews describes how he "refused to be known as the son of Pharaoh's daughter" and "chose to be mistreated along with the people of God." This was a deliberate act on Moses' part to identify with his people. He knew he was taking a risk and that it might cost him his position in the royal family (Hebrews 11:24–26). He was quick to rescue a fellow Hebrew from being beaten by an Egyptian, killing the Egyptian in the process. His motive was right. The problem was that he chose the wrong moment and the wrong method. His abortive and misguided attempt to help his people backfired and he had to flee for his life into the desert. Any hope of saving his people, let alone bringing them back to the Promised Land, faded away. He realised it was an unrealistic dream. But forty years later, he had a dramatic encounter with God, who announced that he was going to intervene to save the people and was sending him back to Egypt.

Moses was given the mandate to set his people free and take them to Canaan. Initially, he was reluctant to answer God's call. He had lost his self-confidence and doubted if he was the right person for the job. But God reassured him that he would always be with him and would enable him to perform miracles. Strengthened by God's promise and encouraged by the support of his brother, Moses realised that the lost dream of his youth might become a reality after all.

This renewed vision of freedom for his people became Moses' all-consuming passion. Everything he did from this moment was focused on leading the people into Canaan. He risked his life as he began the titanic struggle with the king of Egypt. He faced criticism, rejection, hardship and misunderstanding, but it was all with the Promised Land in mind. As he led the people out of Egypt, through the Red Sea and through the wilderness struggling from one crisis to another, this was the vision which sustained him.

Two years after their liberation from Egypt and less than two weeks after leaving Sinai, Moses and his people arrive on the very edge of the Promised Land. They are about to enter the inheritance promised to their ancestors. What a moment for Moses. His vision is about to be realised. Doubtless, for other reasons, Moses looks forward to finally reaching the land. No more sleeping on the hard desert floor. No more trudging through the pitiless desert. No more wearing the same clothes month after month with no washing machines and a shortage of water. No more diet of manna and occasional quail. No more packing and unpacking. Instead, they will soon have a decent bed, a permanent home, fresh fruit and vegetables and the possibility of a cold dip in a refreshing mountain pool. Moses too is probably looking forward to a nice place in an old people's home for retired prophets.

His life's work will be complete! He will have achieved all that God has asked of him. The people of Israel will be a free nation in their own rich and fruitful land. It is going to be a glorious end to his ministry. Like Martin Luther King Jr., Moses can say: "I have a dream," and soon that dream will be fulfilled.

When leaders lose their vision

With Canaan in sight Moses, at God's command, sends a team of twelve to explore the land. They come back with a report that the place is as wonderful as he has imagined. The team even bring back huge bunches of grapes to prove the point. It is a land flowing with milk and honey, just as God has promised.

Moses is delighted with what he hears, but his joy is short-lived. The team continues: "Yes, the land is great, but there are lots of people there already, and they are hostile and well equipped. Their cities are well built and well defended. The people are very tall and physically strong. By comparison we feel like grasshoppers. We cannot possibly overcome these people. There is no way we can capture their cities. The task is hopeless."

As the people listen to this report, they are stunned and paralysed by fear. They can only think about the difficulties that lie ahead—the size of the population, the number of tribes, and the strength of the cities. They focus on the problem and forget the promise. God has assured them many times that he will give them their own homeland. That is the central promise of the covenant God made with Abraham, when he declared: "I will give the whole land of Canaan to you and your descendants as an everlasting possession" (see Genesis 17:8). Perhaps as God's people today, both as individuals and as congregations, we fail to move ahead with a vision because we focus on the problems rather than the promises of God's word.

In Numbers 13:27 the people speak of Canaan not as "the land which God will give us" but as "the land to which you sent us." Canaan is no longer seen as the land of promise; it is just the land which Moses tells them to investigate. They no longer believe the promise and, even if they remember it, they doubt if God is able to keep it. They have forgotten what God did for them in Egypt. They have forgotten how God rescued them when they were cut off by the Red Sea and were in danger of being massacred by the Egyptian army. They have forgotten how God met all their needs in the desert and enabled them to defeat the Amalekites.

The reason the people fail to enter the Promised Land is not that they are sinful. It is not because they are weak and inadequately equipped. It is not because they are guilty of idolatry and immorality. It is because they do not believe that God can do what he has promised to do. They fail not because of their sinfulness, but because of their faithlessness.

So, they lose the blessing God wants to give them. They plan to choose a new leader and go back to Egypt. Apparently, they prefer to return to slavery rather than risk their lives in an attempt to enter Canaan. At least, in Egypt they will be safe and alive. But God will not allow them to do that. At first, he seems even intent on destroying them but, in response to Moses' prayer, he spares them. Only the ten spies, who bring such a discouraging report and persuade the people to abandon God's plan for them, are struck down by a plague and die (14:36–37). The rest of the population wander in the wilderness for forty years until they die too and a new generation is born.

It is tragic to consider how the people lose all the blessings God has in store for them. What about us? How many blessings do we fail to receive as Christians because we do not believe God's promise? We may fail to receive the peace of forgiveness because we do not believe his promise of forgiveness. We may worry about our families or our future because we do not trust that our lives are in God's hands. We may never witness the breakthrough in ministry we long for because we do not believe it will ever happen.

How to respond to disappointment

The vision is lost and the invasion of Canaan is put on hold. Moses' dream is blown away. The very thing he has lived and worked for proves to be beyond his grasp. Moses experiences a bitter moment of disappointment. Most of us experience times of disappointment. Sometimes we are disappointed by our friends or by attitudes we encounter in our church. If others do not share our vision and are unwilling to change to meet new challenges, it is easy for us to become discouraged even to the point of leaving the church and looking for another fellowship that shares our vision of what a church should be.

This is the proposition God offers Moses: "Are you fed up with these people, Moses? So am I. They just treat me with contempt and they have no faith in what I can do. Let us leave them where they are. Let them wander around in the wilderness for the next forty years. They are going nowhere. Forget the Children of Israel. Let us start a new denomination. Let us call it the Children of Moses." This is a tempting offer. From one perspective Moses would have been relieved to be rid of this complaining, critical, faithless bunch of people. Perhaps you have felt the same about some members of your church. Moses turns this offer down, and he does so for three good reasons.

Firstly, he still believes the vision God has given him. These people are still God's people. One day they will get to the land. It may not be tomorrow. It may be in forty years' time. But, one day, they will get there, because God has promised they will, and God keeps his promise.

Secondly, Moses cares passionately for God's reputation. He has stayed with these people because of his love for God. He argues: "Lord, this is not going to enhance your reputation. You have taken a people out of Egypt with all kinds of extraordinary signs of power. You have publicly associated yourself with them and adopted them as your people. Now you plan to dump them in the desert. That is not going to push up your popularity ratings. Either people will say you could not finish the job, or they will assume you are not reliable. I do not want people saying these things about you" (see 14:13, 16).

Thirdly, Moses is still committed to God's people. They are the people he has been called to pastor. They have many faults and weaknesses, but they are God's people, and Moses has been appointed to be their shepherd. Whether they are responsive or not, whether they are spiritually alive or unbelieving, he will remain with them. They are constantly giving him a hard time, but they are the people of God and he still loves them. So, he stays and, in so doing, reflects the heart of a true pastor.

THE TRAP OF PERSONAL SIN AND TEMPTATION
(16:1-18, 20:1-13)

Moses has survived one crisis, but soon faces another. A group of four individuals, led by a man called Korah, jealous of the role and status enjoyed by Moses and Aaron, instigate a rebellion. Together with two hundred and fifty well-known council members they rebel against Moses' leadership. God intervenes dramatically. The ringleaders and their followers are destroyed—the ground under them splits apart and swallows them—and Aaron and the priests are reaffirmed in their respective roles (16–18).

This revolt is not the end of opposition to Moses' leadership. In the fortieth year of their wilderness wanderings, just before the beginning of the conquest of the East Bank of the river Jordan, a further crisis erupts when the Israelites face another critical shortage of water. This moment proves to be the lowest point in Moses' life and ministry. He fails to do as God tells him and, as a consequence, loses the privilege of leading the children of Israel into the Promised Land (20).

By now Moses is an old man nearing the end of his life. For four decades he has borne the strain and burden of leading the people and faced their constant criticism. Forty years in leadership is a long time. As I read Numbers 20, I get the impression of Moses as a weary old man who lacks the energy he has in his younger years. He has given his best and has worn himself out. He does not show the patience previously when dealing with troublemakers.

The people have travelled from the desert of Zin to Kadesh Barnea, where they were thirty-eight years earlier. This is the place from which spies have been sent out and came back with such a discouraging report that the Israelites gave up any hope of setting foot in the Promised Land. Moses would have had all those years to reflect on what has happened and to dwell with some degree of regret, perhaps even bitterness, on what might have been. Perhaps he asks himself how he could have handled the situation differently.

You may feel sympathy for Moses. You may have been in the same place yourself. You may look back with pain at things which have happened and feel sad they did not work out better. You may feel burdened with a sense of failure. Or it may just be that you cannot understand why things turned out the way they did, and you honestly cannot see how there could have been another outcome. It is always tempting to look back on things that have not worked out well and to ask what went wrong. It is tempting, but not usually fruitful.

Moses has something else on his mind too. His sister Miriam has just died. The death of his sister may have affected Moses' mood and perhaps it is one of the reasons he acts as he does on this occasion. Miriam is the first of the three—Moses, Aaron and Miriam—to die. God has said that none of that generation would enter the Promised Land. Miriam's death is followed by Aaron's, recorded in verse 28. The death of Moses before he could cross over into the Promised Land is implied in verse 12. It all makes for sombre reading. All three are kept out of the land, at least in this lifetime.

How did Moses fail?

Moses is exasperated by the children of Israel and their constant bickering and criticism. He has had as much as he can take. He faces yet another delegation with more demands and complaints (2). This time the crowd are feeling so desperate that they wish they have died like those struck down by God after Korah's rebellion (Numbers 16). It is an ugly, even dangerous encounter. Moses and Aaron feel they cannot handle the situation and withdraw to seek God's help.

As the duo fall face down in God's presence, they receive instructions on what to do. The solution God gives is not identical to the one he gave in a similar situation in Exodus 17. There Moses was told to strike a rock and, when he did so, water flowed out of the rock. Here he is only told to speak to the rock and it will pour out water. Moses needs to believe that the word of the servant of the Lord will have the same impact as a word spoken by the Lord himself.

God does not always act in the same way. In the history of the church there have been so many different ways in which God has moved among people and brought rapid growth. We must not limit God by expecting him to repeat what he has done previously. Rather we always need to be ready for him to work in new and sometimes surprising ways. God expects us to grow in trusting him. He expects to see spiritual growth even in a man who is about one hundred and twenty years old.

As instructed Moses gathers the people. However, disregarding God's words, he does not speak to the rock. Instead, he strikes the rock in the same way he did before (Exodus 17:1–7). For this he is severely criticised and told that as punishment he will not lead the people into the Promised Land. What exactly has he done wrong? What is the nature of his sin? The text is not explicit but there are some indications of what lie at the heart of his failure.

Why did Moses fail?

A lack of compassion: Moses appears to have lost his temper with the people. He calls them "rebels". The Hebrew word "morim" is not dissimilar in sound and meaning to our word "morons." Psalm 106:33 says that "rash words came from Moses' lips." In a fit of exasperation and frustration, he expresses how angry he feels. We may have some sympathy for him as we are sometimes be irritated by those around us. We do not like their attitudes, their ingratitude or their self-centredness. We too can lose our sense of compassion. We no longer act out of love but out of anger. God still cares for the needs of his people and is compassionate, but on this occasion Moses is not.

A lack of obedience: God has told Moses to speak to the rock, but Moses "rebelled against" this command (Numbers 20:24). It is vital that those who call others to obey God's word set an example. It is critical that those who teach the word of God obey it. A well-known evangelical leader and teacher, who was a household name among Christians in his own country, held crusades all over the world, appeared frequently on television, and wrote a number of popular devotional books. But over a period of seven years, he had an adulterous relationship with a member of his crusade choir. When he met with a road accident, his wife, who was beginning to become suspicious of his affair, sensed that it was a warning from God. The leader took no notice but was eventually discovered in a hotel with his mistress. His closest friends who found him in the hotel were devastated, as was their whole Christian community. Sadly, the leader showed little sign of repentance and began to criticise his former colleagues and accuse them of betrayal.

Whatever our role in the church, our example is of critical importance. The greatest impact Christians can have lies not in their words or their service, but in their example—their faith, their prayer life, their passion and their obedience.

A lack of faith: The rabbinic interpretation of verse 6 is that Moses and Aaron run away from the crowd because they are afraid. At that moment they are not sure God will look after them, even though he has done so before. So, they panic and run into the Tent of Meeting for shelter. Whether or not they believe that God will protect them, they certainly do not believe that they can just command a rock to produce water. They know that in the past Moses has struck a rock and water has come out. In that case they may just have been guided by the Lord to find a weak spot in the rock's surface. But to start talking to rocks is a different ball game. After all, if nothing happens, they will begin to look rather stupid.

Yet this is precisely what God commands Moses to do (verse 8). He wants to stretch Moses' faith, to take him further than he has gone before. He does not want Moses simply to repeat a miracle. Rather, he is seeking to increase the level of Moses' trust in his power to do the seemingly impossible. If striking rocks to produce water is child's play in the realm of miracles, then talking to rocks to get the same effect is like moving things up to post-graduate level.

Are we prepared to hear the Lord telling us to do something we have never done before, to walk a path we have never gone before, to attempt something we have never attempted before? Do we restrict God to the level of our previous experience? Do we shape our expectation of what God will do in the future based on what he has done in the past? In this instance, it appears that Moses does not trust God or regard his words as trustworthy. He is implying that God is not reliable, and so dishonours God.

A lack of humility: God's honour certainly is at stake here. But Moses is more anxious about his reputation than God's. He is worried about what people think of him and what he can do. His focus is more on himself than it is on God. When he addresses the angry crowd, he asks them what they think he, Moses, can do: "Shall *we* bring water out of the rock?" Moses seems more concerned to show his power than to reveal the grace and power of God. Perhaps the root of Moses' failure lies in his lack of humility. God says: "You did not honour me. You did not give the credit to me." Certainly, Moses does seem eager to be the centre of attention.

Sometimes Christians put preachers or evangelists on a pedestal and praise them for their ministry. But in so doing they can encourage a sense of pride, which is not helpful for the preachers or evangelists and which dishonours the name of God, to whom alone glory is due.

In our own limited areas of ministry or teaching or service, we too can take credit for ourselves. We can work out of a desire to impress, to make people think how wonderful or spiritually effective we are. We can take the glory which belongs only to God. Is that Moses' fault? Is he focused on himself? Perhaps his failure is caused by a combination of factors—lost love, failure to obey, lack of trust in God and lack of humility.

The consequence of Moses' failure

Whatever is the true nature of Moses' sin, the consequences are disastrous. He loses the fitting climax of his ministry. He never has the joy of leading the people into the Promised Land. What a moment of triumph that would have been, what an appropriate closure to so many years of faithful service.

Sir Alex Ferguson, former manager of Manchester United Football Club, is arguably the greatest manager in the English Premier League. Over a period of twenty-six years, he led his club from mediocrity to become the most famous club in the world, winning thirteen Premier League titles, five FA Cups, and two UEFA Champions League titles. His retirement was marked by huge celebrations and acknowledgement of his achievements. If Moses has led the Israelites into Canaan, he doubtless would have retired amidst similar celebrations and acclamation for all he has achieved, but that would have detracted from the glory due to God, who is the true liberator of Israel. It may also have encouraged Moses to think more highly of himself than he ought to. After all, he is only the servant of the Lord. Perhaps Moses' outburst towards the angry mob is more than just the act of a moment but rather a symptom of what has been going on in his heart for some time. Perhaps this is the fruit of a seed planted long ago and nurtured through the years. Perhaps it is a direct result of living for so long with a people who constantly express disobedience and doubt.

This episode reminds us that our God is a consuming fire. There are numerous examples in the Bible of what happens to God's people if they break his commands and dishonour him. Peter in his first letter urges us to take this aspect of biblical teaching seriously and warns that the judgement of God begins with the household of God (1 Peter 4:17). James also warns teachers that they will be judged with greater strictness (James 3:1).

Moses feels the judgement deeply. He longs to go into the Promised Land. But he is already one hundred and twenty years old and he would have to die some time. It is probably going to be easier for Joshua if Moses is not around. What young pastor wants his gifted and popular predecessor to remain in his congregation. It is also better that there is no grave in Canaan, for it may have become a place of pilgrimage. When the people get near Canaan, Moses goes to the top of Mount Nebo and God shows him the Promised Land (Deuteronomy 34:1–3). Moses sees the inheritance God has promised to Abraham, but he does not enter it—at least not yet. More than a thousand years later he would stand with the Lord Jesus on the Mount of Transfiguration (Matthew 17:1–13). So, he does get there in the end, but it is a long time to wait!

FOR PERSONAL REFLECTION

1. What disappointments have you faced in the past? How did you react to them and what did you learn form them? What advice would you share with others for whom things have not worked out as they had hoped?

105

2. What was the basis of Moses prayer in 14:13–19 and how did God respond to that prayer?

3. Why do you think Moses reacted so strongly when the people asked for water? What was wrong with his attitude and what lessons do you take away from this episode?

4. Why did God treat Moses so harshly? What does that teach us about the responsibility of those who are called into positions of leadership?

Chapter 8

A People in Distress

I was having lunch at the home of one of the elders of a church at which I had been preaching. He shared the struggles he had faced in his Christian life. "How can God allow so much suffering," he said. "I am not sure that I can go on believing." I was initially shocked that someone who had been a church leader for so long was thinking of abandoning the faith, but perhaps I should not have been so surprised. The Christian life is a battle. Jesus never promised it would be easy to follow him, and spoke of opposition and hostility against his followers. He warned us of the temptations we would face along the way and how easily we could be distracted by the lures of the world and the teaching of false teachers.

As a Christian, you will be well aware of the particular stresses and struggles you face in your spiritual pilgrimage. Doubtless there are times when you are unpopular or even encounter hostility because of your faith and the biblical views you express. You will be familiar with the weaknesses in your own character and the temptations to which you are particularly prone. There may be some Christians that you find it difficult to like. You may disagree with them on some point of doctrine or the way they behave. You may feel little concern for them or desire to help them when they are in trouble.

As the people of Israel continue on their journey through the wilderness and approach the Promised Land, they face many problems. They are certainly not popular as they march towards Canaan and suffer numerous attacks along the way. Some opponents seek to mobilise spiritual forces against them through the use of incantations and curses. When that fails, they try the less subtle method of sexual temptation. On top of these struggles the people also have to contend with division within their own ranks.

Numbers 21–34

OPPOSITION (21:1-35)

The multitude of migrants that Moses has led out of Egypt and through the wilderness is a potential threat to any territory through which they pass. As they come near the Promised Land, a number of local kings, on learning about their advance, become increasingly anxious about the impact of having so many people marching through their country.

When the Israelites move forward towards Edom, Moses sends a message to the king requesting safe passage through his territory. The king of Edom refuses to allow the Israelites to go through his land and leads a large army against them. Moses wants to avoid a war with the Edomites whom he knows are the Israelites' distant relatives. They are the descendants of Esau, who is the older brother of Jacob, the ancestor of the Israelites. Moses decides to bypass the country of Edom and leads the Israelite army by another route.

Wherever the people of Israel go, they seek to pass through peaceably. They dispatch messengers ahead of them, requesting permission for passage through the country and promising they would not use the water from wells or steal from vineyards or harvest fields (21:22). They come in peace and always seek to go on to the next territory without causing any problems or offence, but they are attacked by one army after another. They have no option except to fight their way to their ultimate destination. With the Lord's encouragement, they emerge victorious in every battle (21:1–33).

After these victories, the people are poised to enter the Promised Land, but one king stands in their way. Balak, the king of Moab, is threatened by their advance, but he knows his army is not strong enough to defeat the battle-hardened Israelites. So, he resorts to the use of magic and spiritual power. He summons a local prophet, called Balaam, and asks him to pronounce a curse on the invading army.

In an unexpected and humorous turn of events, God appears to Balaam and tells him not to curse the people of Israel but to bless them instead. As Balaam rides his donkey to meet the king of Moab, God speaks to him through the donkey, which seems to be more intelligent than Balaam. The donkey, seeing the angel of the Lord barring its way, refuses to go a step further and is duly beaten by its master. Much to the prophet's surprise, the donkey then starts to speak to him and complains about his beating.

Balaam must have been surprised to hear the donkey speaking with a human voice, but is shocked even further when he sees the angel of the Lord standing in front of him with his sword drawn, barring his way. The angel allows him to proceed on condition that he only speaks to the king of Moab the message that God gives him. On his arrival in the king's palace, Balaam is asked to curse the people of Israel. Even though he attempts to do so on seven occasions and in different locations, all that come out of his mouth are words of blessing for the people of God (22–24).

God's people face both physical and spiritual opposition on their journey to the Promised Land. A thousand years later, Jesus would teach his disciples that they would be engaged in a war with Satan (Luke 21:31–34) and be attacked by religious and political leaders. He says: "Do not suppose that I have come to bring peace to the earth. I did not come to bring peace, but a sword" (Matthew 10:34). He tells the disciples they would face constant opposition. He warns them: "They will seize you and persecute you. They will hand you over to synagogues and put you in prison, and you will be brought before kings and governors, and all on account of my name" (see Luke 21:12).

That was the experience of the first believers in Jerusalem and the apostles as they sought to take the gospel throughout the Roman Empire. It has continued to be the experience of Christians down the centuries as countless men and women died for their faith in Jesus. According to the Centre for the Study of Global Christianity of Gordon–Conwell Theological Seminary, an evangelical seminary in the USA, it is estimated that one hundred thousand Christians die annually for their faith. Just as the people of Israel found themselves involved in conflict as they made their way to the Promised Land, it is inevitable that those who seek to serve God and faithfully proclaim his truth in every generation will face opposition.

A few months ago, Christian students at our local university organised a weeklong mission to share the gospel with fellow students. There was a great response as many of those who attended meetings, confessing their sense of purposelessness in life, wanted to hear what Jesus could offer them. A month later, the Universities and Colleges Christian Fellowship staff worker, who was a member of our home group, shared her joy at attending the baptism of one of those who had come to faith. That was so encouraging, but almost immediately the local humanist society launched a vitriolic attack in the local media, accusing Christians of homophobia and demanding that the Christian Union be banned from the university. The same week, a teenager from our church shared how she was criticised for sharing her faith in a class on religious education. Sadly, in Britain today, anyone who dares to say that there is only one Saviour for the world is opposed and ridiculed.

The story of Balak and Balaam reminds us that the struggles of the people of God do not exist simply at the physical or social level.

In Egypt, God declares victory not only over the king of Egypt but also over the gods of Egypt (Exodus 12:12). In the battle between Moab and Israel, the king of Moab seeks, albeit unsuccessfully, to invoke spiritual powers to defeat his enemy. In his letter to the Ephesians, the apostle Paul opens our eyes to spiritual realities when he says: "For our struggle is not against flesh and blood, but against the rulers, against the authorities, against the powers of this dark world and against the spiritual forces of evil in the heavenly realms" (6:12). Paul reminds us that Satan will seek to oppose our attempts to witness, tempt us to do wrong and do all he can to disrupt our fellowship with the Lord. We should not be surprised or discouraged when we face trials and difficulties in our Christian lives. We are in a battle in the service of our King, and the heat of the battle reminds us of the reality of that struggle.

TEMPTATION (22:1 – 25:18)

Balaam is not allowed by God to curse his people, but he finds other ways to cause trouble and disrupt their journey. He encourages the kings of Moab and Midian to invite the Israelites to take part in pagan worship and to engage in religious prostitution. The book of Revelation refers to "Balaam, who taught Balak to entice the Israelites to sin so that they ate food sacrificed to idols and committed sexual immorality" (Revelation 2:14). This new strategy proves to be highly successful: "While Israel was staying in Shittim, the men began to indulge in sexual immorality with Moabite women, who invited them to the sacrifices to their gods. The people ate the sacrificial meal and bowed down before these gods" (25:1–2).

The consequence of their failure to resist sexual temptation is disastrous both for the Israelites and for their enemies. We read that the Lord's anger burns against the people of Israel and he commands the ringleaders to be executed. In one tragic case, just as the majority of the people are beginning to repent and ask for forgiveness for what has happened, one man openly and unashamedly brings his Midianite girlfriend into the camp to have sex with her. A grandson of Aaron, Phinehas, is so incensed by this flagrant disregard for God's law that he goes to the tent where the couple are engaging in intercourse and kills them both with a spear (25:6–9). Later, in chapter 31, we read that every Midianite woman who has taken part in this act of communal debauchery is put to death.

We may be shocked by many aspects of this story which reflects a culture and a time in history very different from our own. The Old Testament scholar, John Goldingay, provides a helpful commentary on this passage. He argues that while the first part of this chapter closes with the instruction to kill so many people, "it never says this actually happened." He goes on to point out that in other places in the Old Testament, "the commission to execute people can be more a statement about the terrible nature of their offence than a prescription for a court to implement."[1] Whether or not these sentences are carried out, the events underline how God expects his people to behave and how he views immoral behaviour.

The ability to feel attraction to the opposite sex and to make love is a precious gift from God, but it can so easily be misused or abused. The sobering story about the Midianites demonstrates the importance of personal holiness in the lives of God's people. We are called to be holy in thought as well as deed. We need to be ruthless in dealing with temptation and to take practical steps to avoid situations where we know it will be hard to resist.

We can all be tempted by the things we see and hear. Instead of rejecting them, we may go on thinking about them. We know in our hearts we should not respond to the temptation, but the more we look, the more inviting it seems. Doubt, desire and ambition are three areas

---

[1] John Goldingay, *Numbers and Deuteronomy for Everyone*, p.85.

where we are all tempted and those temptations can seem overwhelming. So, how do we cope? What resources are there to help us?

Firstly, we need to remember that we are not unique: We are not the only people in the world who have faced a particular temptation. Paul tells us: "The temptations in your life are no different from what others experience" (1 Corinthians 10:13, New Living Translation). Jesus knows how hard a struggle it can be, especially if the temptations keep coming back and we feel weak and vulnerable. The writer of Hebrews encourages us: "For we do not have a high priest who is unable to empathize with our weaknesses, but we have one who has been tempted in every way, just as we are—yet he did not sin" (Hebrews 4:15).

Secondly, we need to remember we are not alone. We have received the Holy Spirit to help us produce the fruit of holiness in our lives. Paul tells us that if we walk in the Spirit, we will not fulfil the desires of the flesh (Galatians 5:16). We cannot make ourselves more holy or pure, but if we allow the Spirit to fill our lives, we will find our desire to sin will diminish. Jesus not only understands what it is like to be tempted; he is present to help us. As the writer to the Hebrews says: "Because he himself suffered when he was tempted, he is able to help those who are being tempted" (2:18), and "he is able to save completely those who come to God through him, because he always lives to intercede for them" (7:25).

Thirdly, we need to remember that the temptation will not go on forever. Paul teaches us that we can trust that God will not let us be tempted more than we can stand (1 Corinthians 10:13). He will always be there to help us overcome the temptation. We will go through hard times of temptation but as we seek to stand firm and resist the devil, he will leave us, just as he leaves Jesus after tempting him in the wilderness (Luke 4:13).

DIVISION (26:1 – 36:13)-

Christians face opposition from the world and temptation in their own hearts. They may also experience conflict with their fellow believers. Before Rosemary and I went out to Ethiopia as missionaries, we were warned that our biggest problem in relationships might not be with those we were trying to reach with the gospel but with our fellow missionaries. For a time that proved to be the case.

Sadly, the history of the Christian Church has been marked by conflict and disagreement among those who claimed to follow the same Lord. A major division occurred when the Eastern Orthodox Church split from the Roman Catholic Church in 1054 AD. Five hundred years later, the Reformation led to a further division in the global Christian community with the formation of Protestant churches. Since then, Christians have continued to disagree about doctrine, style of worship and patterns of church organisation, with the result that innumerable new churches have been established and new denominations formed. Some suggest that there are about thirty thousand different Protestant denominations in the world today.

But the problem of division among God's people is not new. As the book of Numbers draws to a close and the people of Israel get nearer to their destination, two issues spark feelings of anger and dissent. In the first, five daughters of a man called Zelophehad are concerned about their family's property. Their father has died leaving no sons and, therefore, no heir. The daughters are naturally troubled about their inheritance rights and the preservation of their father's name in the land. They come to Moses and point out that their father has been a loyal member of the community and therefore they ask why his family should be penalised for the lack of an heir. They recognise that he belonged to the generation who refused many years before to believe that God could enable them to take the Promised Land. This may be why they say: "He died for his own sin" (27:3).

The five daughters assert that, unlike their father, they believe God's promise and are convinced the people of Israel would enter the land. When that happens, they do not want to be disinherited. They continue: "Why should our father's name disappear from his clan because he had no son? Give us property among our father's relatives" (27:4). When Moses consults God about this matter, God declares that the women must be given their inheritance in the land. The final chapter of Numbers provides a footnote to this story and records how the daughters of Zelophehad do inherit their father's land and keep it within the immediate family (36).

The many laws given in the early books of the Bible do not cover every eventuality in life. It is inevitable that circumstances would arise for which there is no clear instruction. The implication is that sometimes common sense must prevail. While Moses had the unique privilege of speaking to God face to face, Christians today have the Word of God to read and the Holy Spirit to guide them. There may be times when we experience amazing, even miraculous guidance, but at other times, God expects us to be guided through our knowledge of Scripture, the promptings of the Holy Spirit, the wisdom of our friends, and plain common sense.

Zelophehad's daughters had been treated unfairly. Although they were speaking on their own behalf when they approached Moses there must have been many families without sons to inherit the family property. Therefore, the case in question was an important social issue, which would affect many families. There was something wrong in the legal system which needed to be corrected. Today, more than ever, we are aware of the way in which, down the centuries, women have been abused, deprived of their rights and treated unjustly. God's people should seek to protect those who suffer any kind of injustice or are being abused by the system.

The second episode which has the potential to cause friction among the tribes also concerns the inheritance of the land. After the Israelites conquer the territory on the East Bank of the river Jordan, some tribes decide they would prefer to stay on that side of the river. The leaders of the tribes of Reuben and Gad, who have very large flocks and herds, have noticed how the land is particularly suitable for livestock. They come to Moses and ask if they could stay in this area and not go over the Jordan with the rest of the Israelite army.

Moses sees immediately how much friction this could cause among the whole community. He appears to be quite angry. His fear is that if these two tribes fail to take part in the invasion of Canaan, other tribes may also say they do not want to cross over the Jordan. They would be in danger of repeating what happened forty years earlier when the spies brought back such a discouraging report that all the tribes refused to enter, leading to disastrous consequences. The command to enter the land and conquer it was given to the whole nation, all twelve tribes, and there is no reason two tribes should be released from their responsibility to take part in that critical, but admittedly dangerous, military campaign.

Moses asks the leaders of the tribes of Gad and Reuben why they should be allowed to settle down on the East Bank, and enjoy a peaceful existence, while the other tribes have to fight their way through the land on the west side of the river. He rebukes them in the strongest possible language and warns them of the consequences if they refuse to join the others: "And here you are, a brood of sinners, standing in the place of your fathers and making the Lord even more angry with Israel. If you turn away from following him, he will again leave all this people in the wilderness, and you will be the cause of their destruction" (32:14–15).

The leaders of the two tribes accept Moses' rebuke and agree to take full part in the invasion until the conquest is complete, but they want to make preparations for the provision and security of their families who would stay behind on the East Bank. Moses agrees to this, averting a crisis and maintaining the unity of the twelve tribes.

It is never easy to avert potential crises, whether at work, in the church or in the home. Tempers can easily flare, words can be expressed in anger and be misunderstood, and it can take a long time before opposing parties are reconciled. Moses handles both situations wisely and decisively. He understands that everyone must be treated fairly and that unity among God's people must be maintained at all costs. They must not think only of themselves and their own needs. They also need to think about the needs and the feelings of their brothers and sisters. "Let each of you look not only to his own interests, but also to the interests of others" (Philippians 2:4, ESV).

The preparation for the invasion of the Promised Land is now almost complete. The boundaries of the land of Canaan and the extent of the inheritance of each tribe are set down (34). Special provision is made for the Levites (35). Joshua is appointed as Moses' successor. It only remains for Moses, as the final act of his leadership, to make a farewell speech, which turns out to be the very long sermon we find in Deuteronomy.

FOR PERSONAL REFLECTION

1. In what ways have you experienced opposition because of your faith? Why do Christians often face persecution? What advice do you find in the New Testament that encourages you when you face hostility or ridicule, because you follow Jesus?

2. What surprises you about the story of Balaam? Why did God stop him from going to the king and then allowed him to

continue on his journey? What motivated Balaam and why did his life end so tragically?

3. Why did Moses respond to the request of the women so positively and to the request of the tribes of Gad and Reuben so angrily? What lessons can we learn from his responses?

4. Why do you think there are so many Christian denominations? What causes division among God's people and what impact does it have on the witness of the church worldwide?

Section 3

The Way Forward

How Do We Have Hope for the Future?

Chapter 9

Remember A Loving God

As I was sorting through some family photographs, memories of happy and sad times flooded my mind. The photographs reminded me of wonderful times we had enjoyed together and some amazing things which we had all but forgotten. It made me realise how God had blessed us, providing for and guiding us. There is great value in spending time to reflect on the past. Some people keep a diary or a prayer journal, and in later years they are able to look back and recall the things that meant so much to them.

In the book of Deuteronomy, Moses preaches a series of sermons to the people of Israel as they draw near to the end of their forty years of wandering through the wilderness. He starts by reminding them of some key events that took place during that epic journey. He wants them to remember what God has done for them and to show their gratitude by the way they live as his special people. As we read their story, we can be encouraged to reflect on the ways God has shown his love to us. That can inspire us to love him more as we live as his people.

Deuteronomy 1–5

What is your favourite book in the Bible? According to a survey conducted in the UK by the Bible Society in 2016, the most popular biblical books are the gospels of John and Luke, Psalms, the story of Ruth and Paul's letter to the Romans. What is Jesus' favourite book? We are never told this, but the one he quotes more often than any other is the book of Deuteronomy.

The name Deuteronomy means the second law. This may imply that this book presents a new set of laws in addition to those previously given. By the time most Christians have read the first four books of the Bible, they are not keen to be faced with yet another book of laws. They are already tired of laws and are surprised that Jesus is so fond of this book, when he often criticises those who have a legalistic approach to Scripture.

The word "Deuteronomy" occurs in the middle of the book (17:18) when future kings are instructed to keep a copy of this law. But the Septuagint, the first Greek translation of the Old Testament, translated the word as "a second law." Down the centuries this name has persisted, even though it is slightly misleading. In Deuteronomy, Moses is not simply repeating laws already given or adding a new set of rules. What he is doing is applying existing teaching to the new situation the people are facing. Forty years have passed since God gave his laws on Mount Sinai. A whole generation of Israelites have died and the next generation are facing different challenges. They will no longer wander through a desert, surviving on a diet of quail and manna. They are poised to enter a land where they will live permanently. They will build houses and cities, plough fields and gather a harvest. Moses wants them to learn how to apply the words of God in this new context.

As we read Moses' sermons, we may be stirred by his passion as he exhorts the Israelites not to turn away from God. He has lived with these people for forty years and knows their weaknesses and their propensity to drift away from whole-hearted allegiance to God. He understands the temptations they will face when they enter the Promised Land. He is aware of the challenges of moving from a nomadic existence in the desert to a totally new way of life in cities.

These sermons are the words of Moses, but he makes it clear he is not just giving his own advice (1:5–6). He is teaching the people what God has already taught him. The teaching given in Deuteronomy and the other books in the Pentateuch is not thought up by Moses or some wise person. Nor are they a collection of wise sayings, good advice and sensible laws gathered from selected sources in surrounding cultures. The teaching—on the deeds, the character and the commands of God—is from God himself.

These sermons are given by Moses at a specific time in the momentous journey of the Israelites. The brief prologue (1:1–4) gives us the geographical and historical setting. It tells us where the people of Israel are and what events have taken place in the previous few months. They have been engaged in battles with tribes on the east bank of the Jordan and have won a series of spectacular victories. Four decades have passed since they left Egypt.

The author is concerned to record accurately what has happened and when it happened. The children of Israel have travelled through the barren rift valley and reached a point north of the Red Sea and east of the river Jordan. They are now close to the Promised Land. It has taken them a long time to get there. The journey from Mount Sinai (called Mount Horeb in this book) to Canaan is meant to be a journey of about eleven days. We see it has taken them very much longer.

REMEMBER WHAT GOD HAS DONE (1:6–3:28)

Moses does not have the benefit of a camera or a video recorder, but he does want to help the people of Israel remember the blessings they have received. At the beginning of his sermon, he highlights significant moments of the previous forty years, to remind the people of all God has done. He starts by retelling the story at Mount Sinai; he continues by recalling some of the things that took place while they were wandering in the wilderness; he concludes by recounting the recent campaign which has taken place on the West Bank of the Jordan. Telling the story as dramatically as he can, he wants the people to relive some of these critical moments in their history.

Moses has a memorable rhetorical style, as do many great orators. Martin Luther King will always be remembered for his "I have a dream" speech. Barak Obama impressed audiences around the world with the power of his oratory. Both had their own styles and personalities. In Deuteronomy, Moses demonstrates his distinctive style as a preacher. In earlier books, Moses is usually repeating the commands and instructions that the Lord has given. In Deuteronomy, he is preaching to the people to evoke their response and urge them to obedience. He speaks with passion and honesty. He is not afraid to tell the truth or to warn the people of the consequences of disobedience. And he addresses them with affection. He loves these people, even though they have given him a hard time for so many years. He only wants the best for them. He knows they will only enjoy God's blessing if they walk closely with him.

Moses' style can be seen throughout the book. He repeats phrases like "Hear the word of the Lord;" "love the Lord your God;" and "fear the Lord your God," as he encourages the people to trust and obey God (6:4, 13). His rhetorical style is so powerful and effective that it appears to set the stylistic and doctrinal pattern for many of the later historical books. Books from Joshua to 2 Kings share this style and vocabulary. They look to the preaching of Moses in Deuteronomy as being the model to follow and the test of orthodoxy.

At Sinai

Moses starts by reminding the people of the time they met God on Sinai (1:5–18). God made a covenant with them and gave them his law. That covenant formed the basis of their relationship with him. He is the God who saved them from slavery and adopted them as his people. This is through no merit of their own. It is an act of his grace, but he does expect that they will reciprocate his love for them by loving him in return. This understanding of the covenant is reflected through the whole of this book.

The people spent two years based at the foot of the mountain, until God told them that they had stayed there long enough and it was time to move on to the Promised Land. Ahead lay the vision of living in peace and freedom in their own land, a land flowing with milk and honey. But between the vision and its fulfilment was the arduous and dangerous journey of a huge convoy of refugees through the wilderness.

Moses realised he could not lead such a large group of people by himself and he appointed wise and respected men from each tribe to share the burden of leadership. This is obviously so significant an event in Moses' mind that he includes it in this brief overview of the past forty years. He is well aware that the great undertaking to which God called him could not be accomplished successfully without an appropriate organisational structure.

In the wilderness

As Moses continues his story, he recounts the early days of their wanderings through the Negev peninsula—a vast and terrible wilderness (1:19–46). The barren and formidable terrain of this arid desert left an indelible impression on their memories. But within a short while they reached the edge of the Promised Land and sent spies to bring back a report on the land, the people and their cities. The spies returned with evidence of the fertility of the land, but reported that the strength of those who lived there and the size of their cities made any success of invasion impossible.

The people were convinced by what the spies said. Facing such a difficult task, they assumed that God hated them (1:27). They argued that the only reason God had brought them out of Egypt was to kill them. Their fear was groundless. They had very poor memories; they were suffering from spiritual amnesia. God had delivered them before, but they forgot what God had done in the past and so lost their opportunity to enter the Promised Land. That whole generation will pass away before the nation will inherit the land. Only Caleb and Joshua—two of the spies—who appreciated what God is giving them and believed in his promise, will be able to enter. The people made a belated attempt to enter the land in spite of the fact God had told them they could not. This was perverse and had tragic consequences. The opportunity had gone. God's will for yesterday is not necessarily God's way for today.

In Transjordan

The third series of historical events that Moses summarises took place more recently. They focused on the military campaign which had just been completed in the territories which lay to the east of the river Jordan (2–3). This involved conflict with a number of kings, who refused to let the Israelites through their territory, and came out to fight them.

Moses reminds the people of how this campaign came about and how they witnessed the specific guidance of God, who told them when to cross significant boundaries, such as the brook Zered (2:13) and the Arnon valley (2:24). God instructed Moses on where he should go and where he should not. These were precise instructions that made it clear which nations the Israelites were to disinherit as an act of the judgement of God, such as the Amorites (2:24–25), and which nations they were to leave alone (2:5, 9, 19). God was in control of the whole operation; he made the decisions, not Moses.

The Israelites were told to spare Seir because its inhabitants, the Edomites, were related to them. They were descended from Esau, the older brother of Jacob (2:5). They were also told not to attack Moab (2:9) and Ammon (2:19), because the Moabites and Ammonites were descendants of Lot, Abraham's nephew. As the Israelites passed through these territories, they were to approach in peace and not pillage, but buy the food they needed. In spite of this, they were often met with hostility and violence.

When the Israelites made a peaceful approach to Sihon, king of Heshbon (2:26–37), they asked for permission to pass through his territory. Sadly, this was refused, and Sihon came out to fight against them, with disastrous consequences for himself and his kingdom. It may be legitimate to conclude that those who refuse to live at peace with the people of God and who choose to fight against them will ultimately find themselves fighting against God himself.

As the Israelites continued on their march, Og, king of Basham, came down to fight against them (3:1–11). He also was completely routed and his land captured by the Israelite army. His land formed the northern part of Transjordan and marked the extent of the conquest on the east bank. This victory guarded the eastern flank of Israel.

With the east bank conquered, some of the tribes decided to settle there, rather than cross over the river Jordan. Moses tells them of their responsibility to cross the river with the other tribes and see the completion of the conquest first before they returned to their chosen inheritance. He demonstrates wise pastoral leadership and points out the importance of mutual dependence and responsibility within God's people.

In a rather sad closing testimony, Moses reminds the people of his personal desire to enter the Promised Land. He was chosen to lead them to the land and spent the last four decades looking forward to that moment. So he approaches God with humility, and asks if he can enter the land with the people. God's answer is unchanged—no.

In recalling their spiritual history Moses reminds the Israelites of the goodness and power of God. Using all his rhetorical skills he paints a vivid picture of the past to evoke gratitude and inspire confidence in the God who has promised to give them the land of Canaan.

Throughout the Bible, God's people are told to remember what God has done for them. The psalmist sings: "Praise the Lord, my soul, and forget not all his benefits" (103:2). We also need to take care not to forget all that God has done. At the last supper, Jesus institutes the Lord's supper to help us remember his sacrifice for us. As he breaks bread and gives it to the disciples, he explains: "This is my body given for you; do this in remembrance of me" (Luke 22:19). When Paul instructs the Christians at Corinth on the way to celebrate the Lord's supper, he says that as often as they eat the bread and drink the cup, they are retelling the story of the cross (1 Corinthians 11:26). The Lord's supper provides us with a regular opportunity to remember the cross, to marvel yet again at the extravagant love Jesus has shown us. It encourages us to love him in return and to seek his grace to live faithful and obedient lives.

REMEMBER WHAT GOD IS LIKE (4: 1-40)

Moses has given the people of Israel a history lesson, reminding them of what God has done for them in both the distant past and more recent events. He now focuses their attention not so much on the deeds of God but on his character, to show them how wonderful God is and how amazed they should be that such a God wants to have anything to do with them.

Moses reminds the people that God communicates with them because he loves them. He does not leave them guessing as to who he is and what he wishes them to do. He speaks to them through Moses, giving them numerous commands and instructions (4:1, 5, 13). These commands are not the edict of a king who reigns today but will not live forever. They are not the legislative programme of some political party in power one day and out of office the next. They are the words of God who is eternal. They carry his authority.

Therefore, these commands are not open for debate or discussion. They are not optional extras that the people can keep if they feel like it. They cannot change, adapt, alter or modify them (4:2). God gives his commands and expects his people to obey them. He has already made it clear that obedience is a prerequisite for those who wish to avoid his judgment and enjoy his blessing. At the bitter waters of Marah, God said: "If you listen carefully to the Lord your God and do what is right in his eyes, if you pay attention to his commands and keep all his decrees, I will not bring on you any of the diseases I brought on the Egyptians" (Exodus 15:26). He also declared when they arrived at the foot of Mount Sinai: "Now if you obey me fully and keep my covenant, then out of all the nations you will be my treasured possession" (Exodus 19:5).

The people of Israel are not saved by their obedience, but they are expected to reflect their gratitude by their response to God's law. They have been redeemed, so they are called to live as such. In the same way, if we claim to believe in Jesus as our Saviour and Lord, but fail to obey God's law, our faith is meaningless. We cannot assume that because we have been saved it does not matter how we live. We cannot argue that the more we sin the more we demonstrate the wonder of God's grace. Paul answers that kind of thinking in Romans: "Shall we go on sinning so that grace may increase? By no means! We are those who have died to sin; how can we live in it any longer?" (Romans 6:1–2).

If we read the Bible and model our lives on its teaching, people will notice how we live differently from others. Deuteronomy 4:6 says: "Observe them [God's decrees and laws] carefully, for this will show your wisdom and understanding to the nations, who will hear about all these decrees and say, 'Surely this great nation is a wise and understanding people.'" People will be impressed by the way you live and the moral decisions you make. They will realise your priorities in life are different from theirs; you are not motivated by the desire for wealth, comfort and pleasure. They will realise your ethical standards are different from theirs. And even if they criticise you, some may be impressed and come to believe in the Lord.

God lives close to his people

One of the distinguishing marks of the people of God is that their God dwells with them. Moses asks: "What other nation is so great as to have their gods near them the way the Lord our God is near us whenever we pray to him?" (7). Although the people of Israel are not told to go out into the world and make disciples, they are called to be a witness to the God whom they worship. Through the story of the Old Testament, we find a few outsiders who come to faith in the Lord, like Rahab and Ruth, because they sense the presence of God among his people.

Jesus says he will always be present among his people (Matthew 28:20) and he also promises that the Holy Spirit will dwell in us. Many people are drawn to believe in Jesus not through long arguments about theology but because they see something of the presence of God in the lives of Christians. Do the people who know see Jesus in us?

In our modern pluralist society where we are constantly told that every religion is the same, it is helpful to remember the claims of Scripture. While many religions reflect mankind's search for spiritual truth, and some may express similar ethical values, the Bible claims to be God's unique revelation of himself, by which every other claim to truth must be judged. God's revealed truth is far superior to any other truth. God's presence through his spirit is qualitatively different from any other religious experience.

God is great

God is transcendent. Moses describes the scene on Mount Sinai: "You came near and stood at the foot of the mountain while it blazed with fire to the very heavens, with black clouds and deep darkness. Then the Lord spoke to you out of the fire. You heard the sound of words but saw no form; there was only a voice" (4:11–12). It was a terrifying experience as the people saw something of God's glory and heard his voice sounding like thunder. They were very afraid, and would always remember the greatness of God after this encounter.

God is greater than anything else in all creation and he is not subject to the limitations of the material universe. The people saw no physical body of God (15). They only heard a voice. That is why they were not allowed to make an image of God, whether in human form or any other form, because nothing they might create could adequately represent God.

We rejoice to sing "What a friend we have in Jesus," but we should always remember how infinitely great and powerful God is. Even in our minds we should be wary of trying to reduce God to size and create a God in our own image. He is a transcendent God and we should tremble before him. We should not ignore aspects of God's character because they do not fit our picture of what we want God to be like.

God is the creator

In the ancient world many people worshipped the sun and moon. One of the main deities in Egypt was Ra, the Sun God. The people of Israel are at times tempted to worship the gods of nature, so Moses warns them: "And when you look up to the sky and see the sun, the moon and the stars—all the heavenly array—do not be enticed into bowing down to them and worshipping things the Lord your God has apportioned to all the nations under heaven" (19). They are to worship the Creator, not anything in creation.

When we look around this beautiful world and see the grandeur of mountain peaks and the beauty of wooded valleys, from the smallest stream to the mightiest waterfall, from a tiny Alpine flower to the beauty of a kingfisher, our hearts should praise God. As the Psalmist declares: "The heavens declare the glory of God; the skies proclaim the work of his hands" (Psalm 19:1). The danger for the Israelites is that they cannot look beyond the natural world and see the glory of God revealed in creation. We too can be in danger of worshipping things in the material universe rather than the one who made everything.

God is the redeemer

This God, great as he is, chose to free a bunch of slaves who had no possible hope of obtaining their freedom by themselves. The conditions of their slavery were so terrible that Moses compares them to living in a furnace, picturing in his mind, perhaps, not only the physical heat in Egypt, but also the severity of the way they were treated. God set them free and adopted them as his own family (20). More than that, he promised to give them a wonderful inheritance in a land flowing with milk and honey. Yet what he has done for us in Christ is even more wonderful. This story shows how gracious he has been towards us. Like the Israelites, we have been saved from our past, accepted into his family, and given an eternal inheritance.

God did not stop at setting the Israelites free; he did not let them go off and left them to their own devices. He gave them a signed and sealed agreement, pledging he would always be with them to bless and protect them. In making a covenant with the people of Israel he committed himself to them as a man would commit himself to his bride. But just as a husband is jealous for the love of his wife so God is jealous for the affections of his people (24). If they are unfaithful, God says he will punish them so that they will turn from all the evil they are doing and come back to his loving embrace.

God is unique

Has any other god done what God has done? That is the question Moses asks. If you search through the whole of time and the whole of space, he argues, you will never find someone like your God. What God did for Israel was unique. What God has done in Christ is even more amazing.

In our society we are called to show respect to people of all faiths. We may admire their sincerity and their devotion. We may be able to agree with them on the ethical principles they advocate. We share with them a conviction of the importance of faith and the efficacy of prayer. At the same time we must maintain with conviction and humility that there is no one like the Lord our God as revealed in the Old Testament Scriptures and as revealed supremely in the Lord Jesus Christ.

REMEMBER WHAT GOD HAS SAID (5:1–33)

Having reminded the people of aspects of God's character, Moses goes on to remind them of his commands, already recorded in Exodus 20. The wording of these two accounts of the Ten Commandments is almost identical but there are a few significant differences.

One is in regard to the reasons for celebrating the Sabbath day. This command is repeated several times during the construction of the Tabernacle when the people were reminded that they must not carry on with the project on the Sabbath, even though it was the building of a house for God. As God rested after six days in the story of creation, so men and women are commanded to rest after six days of work. Here in Deuteronomy, a second reason is given for observing the Sabbath. As well as praising God for creating the world (Exodus 20:11), they can also worship him for redeeming his people (Deuteronomy 5:15).

The fifth command is also expanded slightly in Deuteronomy. "Honour your father and your mother, as the Lord your God has commanded you, so that you may live long and that it may go well with you in the land the Lord your God is giving you" (16). The people of Israel are about to enter the Promised Land and be established as an independent nation. It is important they understand that a sound national life can be based only on a sound family life.

God made a covenant with the generation who came out of Egypt. He demonstrated his awesome power and spoke to them through Moses (3–5). Now that nearly all the adults who were present at Mount Sinai have died, Moses is stressing the personal involvement of the next generation in the covenant he made there. Their faith is not to be a second-hand affair, something passed on from their parents. It is to be a personal commitment to what happened at Mount Sinai. Their faith must be as genuine and vibrant as if they were there and witnessed the glory of God. In the same way our relationship with God through the Lord Jesus Christ is to be as real as if we were present with the disciples in the upper room or standing on the Mount of Olives as Jesus ascended into heaven.

Moses also emphasises the need for the people of God to go on studying, reflecting on and applying the word of God. They are not meant simply to listen to the words of the Ten Commandments and let them pass in one ear and out the other. Moses says: "Hear, Israel, the decrees and laws I declare in your hearing today. Learn them and be sure to follow them" (1). The people are to be permanent Bible students. In every environment and in each new situation, the principles underlying the instructions in the Word of God will be relevant. They must learn them well so that in each new context they will know what to do and how they should behave.

If we constantly feed our minds on Scripture and use every opportunity to grow in our understanding, then our spiritual lives will be nurtured. The word of God and the Spirit of God will equip us to witness, safeguard us from error, and provide us with principles for guidance.

FOR PERSONAL REFLECTION

1. In 1:8 Moses reminds the people of the promises God made to their ancestors. What are those promises? (See Genesis 12:1–3, 7; 13:14–17; 26:3; 28:13–15; 50:24). How does this encourage us to trust God? Share any promise which encourages you.

2. Why is it important to remember what God has done? Make a list of all the ways in which the Lord has blessed us as individuals, as a church and as a nation.

3. What aspects of the Christian life or witness do you find most difficult? What do you fear? What will help you to overcome your fear?

4. Spend some time thinking of the ways in which the Lord has saved, blessed, guided, corrected and protected you.

Chapter 10

Love God with your whole heart

We use the word love to describe affection, friendship, romantic love, care and commitment. The Greeks had four different words to express different aspects of love. So, when we talk of loving God, what do we actually mean? That is the question that is answered in Deuteronomy 6–11. These chapters begin with the command to God's people to love him with all their heart, soul and strength, and go on to demonstrate what total commitment to him means. There is no place for compromise or half-hearted affection. It is easy for any of us to say that we love God, but these chapters serve as a salutary reminder of what these words actually require of us.

Deuteronomy 6–11

"Hear, O Israel: The Lord our God, the Lord is one. Love the Lord your God with all your heart and with all your soul and with all your strength."

If you go to a Jewish synagogue anywhere in the world, you will hear these words recited during the morning and evening services. They form the high point of any service and constitute the nearest thing to a statement of faith or creed for Jewish people. They are the first words of Scripture that a Jewish child will learn. They would have been the first words Mary taught Jesus. The first word "hear" in Hebrew is *shema*, which means "listen, pay attention, obey," and that is the name by which Jews refer to this passage (6:4). These words are a call to recognise the character of God, to acknowledge his authority, and to follow him in love and obedience.

136

A CALL TO WORSHIP GOD (6:1-4)

Deuteronomy 6:4 calls the people of God to recognise that the Lord is the one who brought them out of the land of Egypt, took them across the Red Sea and through the wilderness, gave them his laws and made them his people. They should worship him and no other. The opening statement consists of four words in Hebrew, which in English can be translated "The Lord our God is the only Lord." The Egyptians worship many gods but, in the Exodus events, God shows that they have no power. The plagues demonstrate the powerlessness of the deities of Egypt, such as Isis, Osiris and Ra. Many centuries later, God declares through the prophet Isaiah: "Turn to me and be saved, all you ends of the earth; for I am God, and there is no other" (45:22).

In our contemporary society, as in the time of Moses, there is a belief in many gods. It is a commonly held view that it does not matter what you believe or which god you worship. It is regarded as arrogant and politically incorrect to say there is only one God, yet that is the unequivocal teaching of both the Old and the New Testaments, and Christians are called to testify to that truth.

A CALL TO LOVE GOD (6:4-5)

God calls his people not just to recognise him but to love him wholeheartedly. When Jesus is asked which is the greatest commandment, he replies: "'Love the Lord your God with all your heart and with all your soul and with all your mind.' This is the first and greatest commandment" (Matthew 22:37–38). The rest of Deuteronomy is a commentary on these two verses. It is true that Deuteronomy contains many laws but, as we have already seen, this book is not essentially about the law God gives to his people but about the love he has for them. It is an agreement between two lovers, God and Israel.

137

The whole book is set out like a marriage certificate or legal document where God demonstrates his eternal commitment to his bride. He is saying: "I will love you, keep you, cherish you and protect you." That is the basis of this relationship. God is not drawing up a prenuptial agreement, which demands guarantees from the bride. This is not a "quid pro quo." This is not cutting a deal. This is not saying: "I will scratch your back if you scratch mine." This is a declaration of unconditional love, where God declares his love, and looks for that love to be reciprocated.

The basis of our relationship with God is not fear or obligation. We do not obey God because we are afraid that he will punish us. We do not serve him because we are his slaves entrapped by one more powerful than we are. We do injustice to the Old Testament if we present the Israelite faith as a legalistic religion. For some Jews it may be that, but that is never God's intention. The people of Israel are to be bound to him in a relationship of love.

What is true for the Israelites is equally true for those who follow the Lord Jesus. Our love is to be total, to involve our whole being, our conscious and subconscious mind. Three words—heart, soul and strength—are used to communicate the totality of our commitment. The heart in Hebrew thought is the seat of the intellect. God's people are to use their minds to love him. The soul is viewed in the Old Testament as the centre of our personality, the place where we make our choices, the seat of our emotions. The word strength refers to all our energy. It reinforces the other two words. All our mental and emotional energy must be directed towards loving God.

A CALL TO OBEY GOD (6:6-9)

How do we show that we love God? Love is not just a feeling, as we learn in the film *My Fair Lady*. There, Eliza is pursued by a suitor who keeps saying that he loves her. She replies: "Don't just say that you love me, show me." On several occasions, Jesus says to his disciples: "If you love me, obey my commandments." Love is a commitment. If you love someone, you show that love by doing things that please that person. A child who loves his mother will show that love in practical ways. A husband or wife will try to do things that his or her partner appreciates. We can show our love for God by doing things that please him, by letting his word direct our lives every day.

God tells his people that his commands should always be on their hearts. They should teach them to their children. They should talk about them when they get up and when they go to bed, when they were sitting at home or travelling. God even suggests that they should tie them as symbols on their hands and bind them on their foreheads (6–8). Jewish people have taken this command literally. They make little boxes—called *tefillin* or phylacteries (Matthew 23:5)—in which they insert passages of God's word. When they pray, they bind these boxes on their left arm (so that God's word is near their heart) and on their forehead (so it is near the seat of their thinking).

God also tells his people to write the words on the doorposts of their houses and the gates of their cities (9). So, Jewish people have traditionally put little boxes with scrolls containing portions of God's word on the doorposts of their homes, and on the doorpost of every room in which people live. The only exception is the bathroom, since you are not meant to live in the bathroom, even though some people seem to! These boxes are called *mezuzoth*. It is not clear whether God intends the people to take his commands literally, but the principle is an excellent one, that the word of God should be the guide for everything we do.

God wants his word to guide the thoughts, words and actions of his people. He wants their whole lives to revolve around it. The word of God is to be studied and lived out in the life of every member of the community. Like the people of God in the Old Testament, we are encouraged constantly to read and meditate on his word. We need to find regular times in the day or in the week when we can read and reflect on God's word. That is a privilege we can enjoy, though we should not assume it will always be the case. One man, imprisoned for his faith, was not allowed to read his Bible. It was taken away from him. He was repeatedly beaten and ordered to deny his faith. He managed to survive by thinking about verses from the Bible. When he found a piece of paper, he would scratch verses on the paper with a piece of charcoal and spend his time reflecting on their truths.

HOW TO LOVE GOD (6:10 – 11:32)

Don't get swept off your feet by affluence

The five and a half chapters from Deuteronomy 6:10 to Deuteronomy 11 spell out what it will mean in practice to love God. The people of God will face many temptations in Canaan that draw them away from their love for God. In the desert they live a simple nomadic lifestyle and there are few things to attract their attention or draw their hearts away from God. They know they are totally dependent on God and are content. Rosemary and I have met Christians in Africa who have a similar contentment, even though they do not have a great many possessions. Their lives are not cluttered with so many other things and they seem more content than most Christians in the West, and their love for God seems more genuine.

Moses knows that once they enter the Promised Land, they will live in houses filled with all kinds of good things they did not enjoy before (6:10–12). They will enjoy a more comfortable lifestyle. That is the experience of British people in the decades after the Second World War. The country was moving out of the period of austerity in the post-war years and beginning to enjoy a level of affluence. In 1957, the then British Prime Minister, Harold Macmillan, declared in a speech in Bedford to his fellow Conservatives: "You've never had it so good."

In subsequent decades, the standard of living has continued to rise and, like Singapore, Britain now enjoys one of the highest standards of living in the world. But the increase in affluence has not drawn us closer to God, rather the reverse. The nation has lost any sense of dependence on God. We have all we need. Our houses are full of possessions. Our lives are full of distractions. Christians can be affected just as much as everybody else. As our materialistic appetite grows stronger, our spiritual appetite grows weaker. In the parable of the sower, Jesus illustrates how the cares of the world can choke our response to God's word (Matthew 13:1–23).

The rest of Deuteronomy 6 is a passionate appeal to serve God. "Fear the Lord your God, serve him only…" (13). Those are the words Jesus quotes to Satan when Satan shows him all the kingdoms of the world and their riches. Keeping God's laws is the only route to success and blessing. In several places in the Bible, God anticipates the questions children may ask and tells parents how they should reply. So in Deuteronomy, when, in the future, children ask why they have to keep these laws, the parents are to tell them that the Lord loves them, has saved them and wants them to prosper and flourish (24).

Don't compromise

Deuteronomy 7 begins with a list of the seven tribes who are living in Canaan at that time. Once the Israelites defeated them, they are to have no association with them. They are not to enter into a treaty or covenant with other nations (2). They have a covenant with God and making a covenant with another nation will be an act of disloyalty to the Lord. But sadly, down the centuries, the people of Israel do turn to other nations. Sometimes they ask Assyria for help against Egypt. At other times they look to Egypt for help against Babylon. Such treaties usually involve making sacrifices to the gods of those nations.

The people of Israel are not to intermarry with the surrounding tribes (3–4). Mixed marriages are not of themselves forbidden; Moses married a Cushite woman (Numbers 12:1). What is forbidden is intermarriage where the bride or groom accepts the pagan beliefs and rituals of her or his spouse. Scripture has no objection to God's people marrying those from another ethnic background, but they should only marry those who identify with the family of God and share their faith.

The Israelites are also to be distinct religiously. When the Israelites enter the land, they will find that it is full of hills dedicated to Canaanite gods, such as Asherah, the mother goddess and wife of the god Baal. All over the land there are images of this goddess, many of which represent her as being naked because she is the goddess of love and fertility. The people of Israel are commanded to destroy these images. God says there is no place for compromise. They are to have nothing to do with their enemy, and to destroy anything which may cause them to compromise their faith (5).

As followers of the Lord Jesus, we too must be careful not to enter into partnerships where our faith or ethical standards may be compromised. We should not marry those who are not true believers in the Lord Jesus. We must take care not to indulge in any practices, however harmless they may seem, which are expressly forbidden in the word of God, such as going to fortune-tellers or mediums. We must also guard our minds lest they become infected with the sexual morality of our secular world.

The emphasis in this passage is on the need for God's people to be holy. "For you are a people holy to the Lord your God. The Lord your God has chosen you out of all the peoples on the face of the earth to be his people, his treasured possession" (6). They are called to be a holy people because God is holy. The nations around will look at the people of Israel and notice they are different. God states that they themselves are not so special: "The Lord did not set his affection on you and choose you because you were more numerous than other peoples, for you were the fewest of all peoples" (7). Therefore, they are to take care to follow the commands of the God who loves them, and they must love him in return.

Don't lose your sense of dependence on the Lord

In Deuteronomy 8 God reminds the people to keep their memories alive (2 and 18). They are to remember all the wonderful things that he has done for them. While they were wandering in the desert, their clothes did not wear out and their feet did not get any blisters (4). They need to be careful, when they reach Canaan, not to start boasting. They are not to claim: "My power and the strength of my hands have produced this wealth for me" (17).

If we are successful in life, business or our career, it is easy to attribute it to our own effort, ability and natural talent. Of course, working hard and making full use of our gifts and abilities will often bring positive results. But, ultimately, it is God who has created us, God who has given us our natural abilities, and God who has chosen to bless our lives. God chose the people of Israel and for forty years they are totally dependent on his provision. The Feast of Tabernacles is given to them to remind them of that truth, and even today Jewish people around the world continue to celebrate what God did for them all those years ago. For a whole week every year, an orthodox Jew will erect a simple shelter of branches and leaves and live in it, as a reminder of how the Israelites lived when they were dependent on God. We too need to remember that we are just as dependent on him. The Lord Jesus taught us to pray: "Give us today our daily bread" (Matthew 6:11).

Don't give yourself the credit

The next section of Deuteronomy continues a similar theme (9:1 – 10:11). Do not give yourselves the credit, God warns the Israelites. Do not say it is all my own work. It is no less than I deserve. God has already pointed out that they are not such a great nation. In fact, they are a tiny nation, one of the smallest and least significant nations on earth (7:7). They should not assume that God did so much for them because they are such virtuous people. They are not to say that they have been blessed because they are righteous. The reverse is true, and to drive the point home, God refreshes their memory on how stubborn and rebellious they have been in the past. When Moses spent several weeks on the mountain talking with God and receiving instructions on the building of the Tabernacle, the people grew bored and wondered what had happened to him. Eventually, they grew tired of waiting and persuaded Aaron, who appeared to have been left in charge, to make them an idol. They brought their gold earrings to Aaron who fashioned them into the shape of a calf. Then they offered sacrifices to the idol and praised it as the god who rescued them from Egypt. They later indulged in a wild party which soon degenerated into a sexual orgy (9:7–21).

When Moses came down from the mountain and saw what was going on, he was furious (Exodus 32:19–20). God had blessed these people in so many ways and they had turned round and behaved like this. They had broken the first commandment: "You shall have no other gods but me." They had broken the second: "You shall not make for yourself any idol or graven image." They had broken the seventh: "You shall not commit adultery." Those who were chosen and blessed more than any other nation had rejected God and his moral standards. They showed no appreciation for everything God had done for them over the past two years.

The covenant, so recently concluded, was broken. Moses threw the tablets of the law onto the ground and they were smashed to pieces. God's covenant with Israel was torn up like a marriage certificate with the ink still wet on the paper. The situation was only saved through Moses' desperate plea for mercy (9:19–20).

In retelling the story, Moses reminds the people of what they did wrong and how God graciously forgave them. We too are reminded that God knows everything we have done. Sometimes it is good to recall the past and remember we are not such wonderful people after all. We may not like to think about the things we have done but it can be most helpful to do so. We can remember how gracious God has been to us and thank him for sending his son to die so that we can be forgiven. The price is paid. The slate is wiped clean. He has loved us so much and he longs for us to love him in return.

Walk hand in hand with God

Moses has been calling the people to love God with all their heart, soul and strength. He has highlighted the temptations and dangers they will face as they enter the land of promise. He has pointed out that they may be tempted to attribute their military success to their own strength. They may assume their increasing wealth is the result of their own ability, and begin to feel they can do without God. They may also be seduced by the practices and lifestyle of the people around them.

Moses now urges them to walk hand in hand with God (10:12 – 11:32). He longs for them to fear, obey and love the Lord. That is the only safeguard against the dangers and temptations which await them once they cross the river Jordan and settle in the Promised Land. They need to determine that whatever happens they will worship only God and always keep his commandments.

Their future is in their own hands. They have a choice to make—to go their own way or to go God's way. Moses lays out the option: "See, I am setting before you today a blessing and a curse" (11:26). Whatever they choose to do will have consequences. That is true in the physical realm, where there is a law of cause and effect. If you jump into deep water when you cannot swim, you will drown. If you drive a car over a cliff, you will almost certainly die. Similarly, there is a law of cause and effect in the spiritual realm. If you obey God, you will enjoy his blessing. If you disobey God, you will experience his judgement. That is not because God does not love you. It is because you are choosing not to love God. Do not blame God. The choice is yours.

The same truth applies to us. By our decisions day by day we are either drawing closer to God or going further away from him. I remember when Dr Helen Roseveare, who served for twenty years as a missionary doctor in the Congo and authored several books, came to the college where Rosemary and I were teaching. She addressed the topic of spiritual maturity. She said that we do not grow to maturity through one momentous spiritual experience, helpful as that may be. We grow towards maturity as we learn day by day and moment by moment to live our lives in the way that pleases God.

Moses pleads with the people to seek to obey God in everything they say and do. Circumcise your heart, God says (10:16). Physical circumcision was suspended during the time in the wilderness. Here God is speaking of a spiritual circumcision of the heart. Everything that may restrict or interfere with their devotion to God is to be cut away. For us too, where there are things in our hearts which restrict what God can do in our lives or negate his lordship, to that extent our hearts are uncircumcised.

This is the vertical dimension of our Christian lives, showing that we love God. But there is also a horizontal dimension to our lives. We are to love our neighbours, whether or not they belong to the people of God. There may be people or groups of people we find it difficult to like, but Jesus says we are to love our enemies. It is while we are God's enemies that he chooses us and draws us to himself. God is the one who defends the cause of the fatherless and the widow, and loves the foreigner, and he expects his people to do the same. "And you are to love those who are foreigners, for you yourselves were foreigners in Egypt" (10:19). We must do the same. Our walk with God is to be characterised by the circumcision of our hearts and a deep concern for the needs of our fellow human beings.

These seven chapters contain one central message—the people are to love God. Loving God means obeying his commandments and allowing his word to guide them in everything they do and say. It means taking care they are not seduced by things around them and do not compromise their faith or their moral behaviour. They must never lose their sense of dependence on the Lord or give themselves the credit for all they achieve. Day by day they are to walk hand in hand with the God who loves them and they are to love him unreservedly in return.

FOR PERSONAL REFLECTION

1. Read Deuteronomy 6:4–5. What do we love with all our heart, soul and strength? What dominates our thinking? What makes our life worth living? What drives our lives and dictates our choices?

2. What practical steps can we take to make sure the Lord remains at the centre of our lives and of our families? How can we become more disciplined in the study of his Word? What are the dangers for Christians of living in a prosperous, safe and well-governed society?

3. In what ways may we be tempted to compromise our faith? How can we maintain a distinct witness while showing respect for others?

4. What do people see when they look at us? Do they see any distinctiveness in the way we live, in our attitudes or behaviour?

Chapter 11

Build A Godly Society

How far should we as Christians be involved in politics and social action? We spend time attending church meetings and we try to share the good news of Jesus with those around us. We know these are our priorities and we may feel we do not have the time or the ability to be involved in the wider affairs of our local community. It is easier to stay within the comfort zone of our Christian fellowship than to engage in local social or community projects with people who may have very different values or moral standards.

As Moses continues his sermon, he reminds the people of the importance of pure devotion and correct teaching. He then makes it clear that God is interested not only in matters of worship but also in issues of justice, social equality and good governance. He is concerned that the leaders of society, those who judge in the courts and those who teach, are faithful and responsible in all they do. The challenge that comes to us as we read Deuteronomy 12–18 chapters is the part we play or should play not only in contributing to the life of our churches but also in helping to build a just and fair society.

Deuteronomy 12–18

We live in a rapidly changing world. The process of urbanisation means that millions of people who grew up with a simple rural lifestyle face the challenge and chaos of city life city. Advances in medical science have confronted society with hard ethical questions on the sanctity of human life and the morality of euthanasia. Natural disasters and unresolved conflicts have forced huge numbers of people to migrate from their ancestral homes to foreign countries where language and culture are strange and confusing.

Communications technology has provided access to untold sources of knowledge and information, some accurate and some fake, has spread a multitude of philosophies, religions, ideas and moral opinions, which are baffling and overwhelming. Children born in the twenty-first century face pressures and temptations their parents find difficult to comprehend.

It is not easy to be a Christian in such a world and to witness effectively for Christ. Each new scientific discovery seems to present yet another challenge to Christian faith and behaviour. In Deuteronomy, Moses warns the people of Israel of the challenges they will face as they enter the Promised Land. How will they cope with these pressures? How will they respond to the new temptations and opportunities they encounter?

This section of Deuteronomy is full of practical advice. Moses seeks to explain what it will mean to be the people of God living in a new and different environment. This is similar to the pattern we find in many of Paul's letters in the New Testament, where he deals with matters of doctrine in the early part of a letter and then goes on to address the practical implications of being a Christian. If Deuteronomy 4–11 speak in broad terms about what it means to love and be totally committed to God, then chapters 12–26 spell out in detail what this means in every area of life.

In the previous three books of the Pentateuch, a large number of laws have been given on different occasions covering a wide range of topics. Now Moses seeks to bring those laws together more systematically. It is similar to a highway code which brings together all the laws relating to the use of roads in a particular country or state. Now the laws given to the people of Israel are brought together in a coherent and logical order, as Moses tackles a broad range of subjects, including work, marriage, family life, leisure, money and communal life. He begins by addressing issues relating to worship and leadership.

WORSHIP (12:1–16:17)

For forty years the people have been in the wilderness. That was a time for spiritual growth, where they could learn the importance of obedience and the consequences of disobedience. It was an unusual learning environment in the way that doing a course in a residential Bible school or spending a week at a Christian camp is not the same as living at home or working in the office.

There is value in having a prolonged period when distractions are not so numerous, pressures not so great, and temptations not so immediate. Many will have experienced the joy and encouragement of a church camp or house-party, where we feel uplifted by the teaching, worship and times of fellowship. We also know that, eventually, we have to return to the harsh realities of the real world and the challenge of living out what we have learned in the workplace. In the same way, the people of Israel are about to move from the isolation of the wilderness into the land of Canaan. They will be surrounded by people who follow different laws, have different moral standards, and worship other gods. Moses points out some key lessons they must remember, lessons which are just as relevant for us living in the confusion of the twenty-first century.

They must worship only one God in the way he prescribes

First, Moses reminds the people that they must only worship God (12:1-32). In Canaan, they will see places of worship dedicated to all kinds of deities. They may be tempted to visit these places and adopt some of their practices. This may lead them to pray to the Lord on the Sabbath and offer sacrifices to another deity on some other day of the week. They must not pray to the Lord for his blessing and then pray to Baal for a good harvest. That is a temptation for the people of Israel, not least because worship at a pagan shrine may include the practice of sleeping with a cultic prostitute.

We may not be tempted to worship at the shrine of another god but we may be tempted to pray to someone other than God, or to visit a medium in an attempt to contact a family member who has died. When Rosemary and I were living in Singapore, we met a lady who regularly went to church, but when her daughter was taking exams, she also went to burn incense at a local temple to seek the help of other gods. In the West, there are people who claim to be Christians but will have a statue of Buddha in their garden. Some go regularly to church, while reading their horoscopes in the newspaper and taking the predictions very seriously.

Moses also makes it clear that they must worship God in the place he chooses and in the manner he prescribes. The Tabernacle is the place where they can draw near to God and find forgiveness for their sins (12:4–6). As Christians, in Jesus, we are privileged to draw near to God. We do not need to offer sacrifice for our sins because Jesus has given himself as a sacrifice for us once and for all time (Hebrews 10:12).

I remember hearing of some Ethiopian Orthodox priests who were used to offering the sacrifice of the mass on a daily basis for themselves and the people. They were amazed when they read those words from Hebrews 10:12 that told them that Jesus had made one sacrifice which was valid for all time. They could scarcely contain their amazement and joy, as they realised that God accepted and forgave them because of what Jesus had achieved on the cross and not because of any sacrifices they offered.

In Philippians 3, the apostle Paul explains how, as an orthodox religious Jew, he had an almost perfect record. He was a zealous defender of the Jewish Scriptures as he understood them. He was righteous in the eyes of the law because he kept the law in its entirety, offering appropriate sacrifice when necessary. Paul's record was as good as anyone else and far better than others in terms of doing good works. But Paul goes on to explain that he knows it cannot save him or make him right with God. Paul understands the only place he can draw near to God is at the foot of the cross.

They must beware of new teaching

If the first danger facing Israel is the presence of pagan shrines, the second is the existence of numerous false prophets, who could lead the people to worship other gods (13:1–2). These false teachers may accurately predict future events or perform miracles, but if they draw the people away from worshipping God, their teaching is to be rejected. In the same way, in the New Testament, the acid test of a true prophet or teacher is whether they give exclusive allegiance to Jesus and acknowledge that he has come in the flesh to redeem them (1 John 4:1–2).

Jesus repeatedly warns his disciples that false prophets will come and lead many astray. We need to be alert to this danger. We hear of respected church leaders who deny the virgin birth, question the miracles of Scripture, refuse to accept the authority of God's word or, like a former bishop of Durham, deny the physical resurrection of Jesus. They are indeed wolves in sheep's (or even shepherds') clothing who can lead God's flock astray and upset the faith of many.

There are also popular teachers and evangelists who promise untold wealth and disease-free living, if only we claim the promises of God by faith. Such teaching sounds appealing but is built on a superficial interpretation of isolated texts and ignores the New Testament focus that our treasure will be in heaven, not untold wealth on earth. To attract people to faith in God through offering material benefit is the problem Jesus faces when thousands come looking for him because he has given them a good meal! Some preachers go around the world advocating one spiritual gift or another as the answer to all our spiritual needs. In every age, we need t0 be aware of false prophets with remarkable gifts and powers of persuasion. We should judge them not on the basis of what they can do, but on the basis of what they teach.

They must reject questionable practices

Self-laceration plays a part in the worship of other gods (14:1). God's people are not to do anything which disfigures the human body or has associations with pagan worship. They are to be different from other nations, not just in their moral behaviour but also in their customs and diet. They are to avoid any rituals based on superstition, such as the command: "Do not cook a young goat in its mother's milk" (21). This law is intended to forbid not a particular recipe but the use of a magic spell. It is a common belief in surrounding cultures that boiling a kid in the milk of its mother will guarantee the continuing fertility of the herd.

In the New Testament, when Paul deals with a question like should Christians eat meat which has been offered to an idol, his concern is the impression the act will give. He argues that although the followers of Jesus do not believe in the power of idols or the existence of the gods they represent, they should not eat meat offered to an idol that offends other Christians or gives the impression they approve of idol worship (1 Corinthians 10:27–33).

They must avoid spiritual apathy

Here the people are told they must be regular in their giving to the Lord. They are to set aside a tithe or a tenth of all their produce every year and take it to the place God chooses (14:22). The purpose of the tithe is to acknowledge their dependence on God (23), to express thanks to him (26), to support the priests (27), and to give to the poor (29).

Deuteronomy 15 expands the theme of caring for the poor and those who have fallen on hard times. It deals with the cancelling of debts and the treatment of slaves. The people are encouraged to be generous and kind-hearted (15:7,10). They must be willing to lend and help those in difficulty. If an Israelite borrows money, the debt must be cancelled in the seventh year (15:1–6). This is to prevent his falling into the poverty trap and being the target of loan sharks for the rest of his life. Even if the year for debt cancellation is drawing near, those who are able to lend to others should still do so, even if the chance of getting their money back is reduced.

These enlightened policies remind the people of God in every generation of the need to be generous, kind and open-handed. If we ask whether, as Christians, we should give a tithe to God, the answer is that, although this command is not explicitly stated in the New Testament, it is difficult to imagine why we should give less to God. We too are to express our thanks to God and our dependence on him. We are responsible to support those in full-time ministry and we have a moral responsibility to help the poor.

In Deuteronomy 16 Moses moves onto another area where we are to be active in maintaining our fellowship with God. He reminds the people to observe the three major religious festivals: Passover, Pentecost and Tabernacles, which we have already considered (16:1–17, cf. Leviticus 23). All the men are expected to come to the Tabernacle. Women too are welcome but if they have small children they may be excused. If observing the festivals involves a long trek it may be tempting for the men to miss a festival on the grounds they are tired or need to spend more time on the farm. Their attendance can become less and less frequent. Moses is warning them not to become

155

half-hearted or erratic in fulfilling their spiritual obligations. Many Christians observe a series of special days or festivals during the course of the year, such as Advent, Christmas, Lent, Good Friday, Easter and Pentecost. While not all may adhere rigidly to a liturgical calendar, every believer will benefit from regularly remembering the great acts of salvation, reminding us who God is and what he has done for us.

LEADERSHIP (16:18–18:22)

In many countries people complain about the way their country is governed. They argue taxes are too high and the government is not providing the services needed in the community. If they live in a democratic country, they will have the opportunity every few years to vote for a new set of leaders. Others have no choice but to accept the governance of the same party for many decades, even though they protest they are treated unfairly, their leaders are corrupt, and it is impossible to get justice in the courts.

In the workplace some employees are concerned about how they are treated by their bosses, who have unreasonable expectations and are not interested in their wellbeing. They may be treated badly but be given little opportunity to express their frustration or ask for better working conditions.

This section in Deuteronomy addresses the subject of leadership in all areas of society. It reflects God's concern for the social, political, economic and religious lives of his people. He wants them to benefit from a fair judicial system, good governance and strong spiritual leadership.

Provision for a supreme court

First, God shows his desire for a just legal system (16:18–17:13). God provides for the appointment of judges in every town so that cases can be heard and decided, criminals duly punished, and communities enjoy peace and safety. These judges must not be corrupt or show favouritism. They must judge fairly: "Follow justice and justice alone" (16:20).

After the death of Joshua, the leadership of Israel falls to a succession of men and women known as judges. This system does not work well. The rule of each judge is restricted in area and in some cases only lasts a short time. The administration of justice in Israel falls largely to local elders who are appointed on the basis of their position and standing in the community. They are required to deal with matters of civil concern and to do so fairly and to the best of their ability. Later in the history of Israel, sadly, the prophets often complain of the utter corruption of the courts where the rich would bribe judges to decide in their favour.

Provision for the appointment of a king

Because of the chaotic situation that prevails at the end of the period of the judges when "everyone did as they saw fit" (Judges 21:25), it seems inevitable that the people will demand to have a king who will provide a more stable system of government. Their motivation for doing so does not please God but he allows them to have their wish and even builds the idea of kingship into his plan of salvation for the world.

God gives clear advice as to how this king should behave (17:14–20). He must not rely on the size of his army and imagine he is invulnerable (17:16). His trust is to be in the Lord and not in his military strength. He is not to multiply wives, as is the custom in other royal courts. Foreign wives can turn the king's heart away from following the Lord, which is precisely what happens to Solomon, who takes countless foreign wives and allows them to bring their idols into the holy city of Jerusalem (1 Kings 11:3–7).

God also stipulates that the king should not amass wealth, as other monarchs do. If that becomes his consuming passion, it can place intolerable tax burdens on his people. Solomon develops a passion for huge building projects all over the country and forces the people to leave their farmlands and work on his projects. The social unrest caused by this policy is one of the main reasons for the division of the kingdom after his death.

Finally, God commands that the king should keep a copy of these instructions. He is to read and study what God has decreed about the conduct of anyone who becomes king. Like his people, he is to live under the authority and guiding principles of God's word.

We are not kings or queens but we may hold positions of authority over others. Whether that authority is over one individual, a small team or an international company, we can all find useful leadership principles in these verses. We should not abuse our power by maltreating those under us or making unreasonable demands on their time. Driven by a desire to make as much money as possible, we should not pay them a pittance simply because they have no alternative but to accept the terms we lay down. Those who are in retail can make huge profits by buying from unscrupulous suppliers who hold their labour force in conditions tantamount to slavery.

Similar lessons can be learned by those who exercise leadership in a church. These leaders too must recognise that they live under God's rule. They must be true believers who know God's word and set a good example to those they lead. They must take care of the flock over which they have been placed as under shepherds. Sadly, not all pastors lead well. Some do not know the Scriptures well and may even teach what is contrary to the truth of God's word. Some exercise an autocratic style of leadership and show little consideration for the feelings of church members. Others dishonour the name of Jesus by the way they behave. Such behaviour tarnishes the witness of the church in the world.

Most church members are not engaged in "fulltime" ministry but they do belong to a local community and are citizens of a nation. God's desire is that all those citizens live in a just and well-governed society. Each of us has the responsibility of playing our part in that society in whatever way we can, either by social action or political involvement. We cannot complain about the way our town or country is governed if we are not prepared to be involved actively in the process of governance. We are not only called to witness to Jesus. We are also called to help build a better world.

Provision for priests and Levites

Priests belong to the tribe of Levi and are members of the family of Aaron (18:1–8). They have positions of authority and honour. They live around the central sanctuary and offer sacrifices. The rest of the tribe of Levi serve as Levites. They support the work of the priests and are subordinate to them. They do not offer sacrifices and they live in cities assigned to them. Both priests and Levites are to instruct the people in the word of God. Neither group are allotted land, so they are dependent on the giving of the people for financial support and their share of the offerings.

The New Testament does not refer to church leaders as priests. The term "priest" is only applied either to the Lord Jesus as our great High Priest or the whole community of God's people, all Christians, who are described as a kingdom of priests (1 Peter 2:5–9). In the same way that the people of Israel are responsible for providing for the physical needs of the priests and Levites in Old Testament times, all Christians share the responsibility of supporting the work of ministers and missionaries. The New Testament makes it clear that those who serve as evangelists, pastors or teachers should be provided for by the people of God (1 Corinthians 9:13, 1 Timothy 5:17). Paul refers to Deuteronomy in support of his argument (Deuteronomy 25:4). Even though he, at times, does not insist on his right for financial support as an evangelist, he strongly argues that others in similar ministry should be fully supported.

Provision for prophets

The surrounding nations have many magical and superstitious practices to help them discover the will of their gods. They practise divination or sorcery, observe the stars, watch birds, look at the entrails of sacrificed animals, mix magic potions, pronounce spells and consult the dead. The people of God are not to engage in any of these practices. God promises that from time to time he will send a prophet to bring his word to his people (18:9–10), and he does so, with a succession of godly men and women (2 Kings 22:14, 2 Chronicles 34:22, Isaiah 8:3).

As time passes, there is a growing expectation of one special prophet who will come to bring God's word. In many people's minds that prophet becomes associated with the coming of the Messiah. Moses speaks of the coming of such a prophet, a prophet who will be raised up by God and speak with his authority just as Moses does (18:18). Many centuries later, John the Baptist is asked if he is that prophet (John 1:21). He refutes this suggestion and points his questioners to Jesus.

We now have the words of all prophets recorded in the Bible. We do not need to resort to any of the bizarre and dangerous practices which are explicitly forbidden in Deuteronomy. We can learn about the will of God from the writings of those who, inspired by the Holy Spirit, teach us what we should believe and how we are to behave. These Scriptures also help us to appraise the words of those who teach us and to discern truth from error.

While bands of prophets do not wander around our cities today in the way they did in ancient Israel, we do have many who exert huge influence in moulding societal opinion. These include teachers, politicians, news reporters and those who operate through the media. In today's postmodern world, Christians need the ability to discern the difference between human opinion and the truth that God has declared.

Deuteronomy 16–18 describe the kind of leaders through whom God seeks to provide for his people a fair judicial system, good governance and strong spiritual leadership. Some of those, who are chosen to serve as judges, kings, priests or prophets, seek as best as they can to fulfil their calling. Many will fail: judges become corrupt, kings turn away from God, prophets prophesy lies and priests kill the innocent (Isaiah 56:10–11, Jeremiah 5:31, Lamentations 4:13).

God recognises that all leaders are fallible and can make mistakes, but he promises that one day he will send someone who will perfectly fulfil the role of judge, king, prophet and priest (18:15-18). He is the one who will judge all people. He will not judge by what he sees, or decide by what he hears, but with righteousness he will judge the needy and with justice he will give decisions for the poor of the earth (Isaiah 11:3ff.).

He is the king whose name is Wonderful Counsellor, Mighty God, Everlasting Father, Prince of Peace. Of the increase of his government there will be no end and he will reign on David's throne and over his kingdom from that time and forever (Isaiah 9:6–7). He is the priest after the order of Melchizedek, who lives forever and who is able to save completely those who come to God through him, because he lives to make intercession for them (Hebrews 7:1–28). He is the prophet, like Moses, sent by God to bring his word to his people. He is like Moses, but so much greater than Moses. Moses is a servant, whereas Jesus is the Son (Hebrews 3:1–6). Moses brings the word of God. Jesus is the Word of God (Hebrews 1:1–4, John 1:1–18).

FOR PERSONAL REFLECTION

1. What pressures do Christians in your country face in the twenty-first century to conform to contemporary culture?

2. In what ways are we in danger of spiritual apathy or laziness? How can we correct that?

3. What lessons might be learned from Deuteronomy 16–18 by anyone who exercises power or leadership either in the secular world or in the church?

4. What is the role of prophets in the church today? How do we know when a message is genuinely from the Lord (13:1–5, 18:9–22, 1 Corinthians 12:7–11, 14:29–33, 1 John 4:1)?

Chapter 12

Make the right choice

We have to make many choices during our lives. Some are trivial and insignificant. Others are major decisions impacting the course of our lives. In his final address to the people of Israel, Moses tells them it is time to make their minds up. They have to choose whom they will serve. Over the months and years, Moses has been preparing the people for the new life that awaits them in the Promised Land. He has told them of the many good things they will be able to enjoy in Canaan, but he has also warned them of the dangers and temptations they will face. Before they cross the Jordan and enter the land, they must decide once and for all whether they are going to live a life in obedience to the laws God has given or ignore his commands and go their own way.

The closing chapters of Deuteronomy confront us with a similar challenge. Are we tempted to make our own choices without any reference to God? Or are we determined to be totally committed and loyal to Jesus? Will we be among those who choose to serve the Lord with our whole hearts? Will we be like Joshua, who proves his faith and commitment to God, and is appointed as the successor to Moses? Will we be like Moses, a man who has served God faithfully for forty years and lived so close to God that he is described as the one whom "the Lord knew face to face"?

Deuteronomy 19–34

God lays down a set of laws for his people because he loves them and wants them to live long in the land he is giving them. Through his laws, he teaches them how to live in a way that reflects his character. How are these laws relevant and applicable to us today? We know all

Scripture is inspired by God and is written for our benefit (2 Timothy 3:15–16), but how do we discern which laws we are to follow?

Some Old Testament laws no longer apply to us as Christians. We are not bound to observe the dietary laws because the New Testament teaches us that all food is clean (Mark 7:19). It is no longer necessary for us to offer sacrifices for our sins because Christ has offered his life as the one perfect sacrifice for all time. We no longer need to go to a Tabernacle or Temple to worship God, for now we can draw near to God in any place and at any time through the Lord Jesus.

Some laws do not apply to us directly because they have been given to Israel as a nation. A law given to the nation of Israel cannot simply be transferred to the Christian church, but the principle underlying the law may still have relevance for us today. In the Mosaic law, severe penalties were prescribed for those who flagrantly flouted God's law and committed murder, theft or adultery. Christians would regard such behaviour with the utmost seriousness and consider that those who commit such crimes should be called to account. In 1 Corinthians Paul argues that a man who persistently disobeyed God's law and refused to change his behaviour, should be asked to leave the church, in the hope that might lead him to repentance (5:13).

As we consider any law, we must ask questions to discern what kind of conduct the law is trying to prevent or promote. What kind of people will it protect or restrain? What principles can we deduce which we can apply in our modern context? It is not possible to look at all the laws in detail, but even a cursory reading of Deuteronomy 19–34 reveals several major themes.

GOD IS CONCERNED FOR JUSTICE (19–21)

We read, first, that God desires justice in the courts in cases of manslaughter and murder (19). It starts with an example of manslaughter where a man is cutting down trees and his axe head flies off the handle and kills someone. Even though this is an accident, the person involved may be afraid that the relatives of the dead man will seek revenge. They will inevitably be angry and may want to take the law into their own hands (6). To safeguard the innocent, Moses sets aside six cities of refuge in different parts of the country. Anyone who is guilty of manslaughter can flee to any of those cities and safely remain there until the death of the High Priest (Numbers 35:25). It is believed that the High Priest's death serves to expiate his blood guilt. We are not told how the death has this effect but it serves as an amazing pointer towards the Lord Jesus.

In the case of premeditated murder (11–13), capital punishment is deemed appropriate. Although severe punishments are frequently prescribed, including the death penalty, there are very few examples where such punishments are exacted. God is seeking to teach his people the sacredness of human life and the seriousness of sin.

Moses goes on to deal with cases of perjury and false witness (14–21). Due process of the law must be followed and all charges thoroughly examined. Evidence given must always be confirmed by other witnesses. There is always the danger that witnesses may fabricate evidence because they are bribed to do so or may act out of malice towards the accused. In a murder trial, much depends on the testimony of witnesses. Those found guilty of perjury are condemned to suffer the same fate as the one condemned on their evidence (18–19).

Disputes about property and land ownership frequently occur in every culture. In ancient Israel, a common practice involves moving a neighbour's landmark to extend one's own property (14). This may not seem such a serious crime as murder, but it could have grave consequences, reducing the size of a land and depriving the owners of the ability to support the whole family.

God also sets down guidelines for fair and just behaviour in the conduct of war (20:1–20). He is concerned for the welfare of those who serve in the army and for the civilised treatment of their enemies. With the exception of those tribes that God has already condemned, the Israelites are to spare the inhabitants of any city willing to surrender. They are to treat their prisoners humanely and with respect (10–18). They are not to destroy the enemies' olive groves, vineyards and date palms, even though such behaviour is common practice in the ancient world and still occurs today (19–20). They are also commanded to treat female prisoners of war with respect. A soldier is not to rape or enslave one of these prisoners, but if he wishes to marry her, he has to grant her the full status of a wife (21:10-14).

Christopher Wright makes the following perceptive comment on these laws: "Without a Geneva convention, Deuteronomy advocates humane exceptions from combat; requires prior negotiation (before the commencement of war); prefers non-violence; limits the treatment of subject populations; allows for the execution of male combatants only; demands humane and dignified treatment of female captives; and insists on ecological restraint."[2]

THE NEW SOCIETY (22–26)

Towards the end of his long sermon, Moses describes his God-given vision of a new society. He wants the people to live in harmony, to be good neighbours (22:1–4). If they see their neighbour's ox or sheep wandering around, they should take it back to its owner or keep

---

[2]Christopher Wright, *Deuteronomy, NIBC* (Peabody, Mass.: Hendrickson, 1996), p. 230

it safe till the owner is found. They should not ignore the problem and assume it is none of their business. God's people should care for each other.

They should also care for the environment and, in particular, conserve the resources of the natural world (22:6–7). One example given is that of a person finding a nest, where a bird is sitting on eggs. The person is allowed to take the eggs but must leave the bird so that it can lay more eggs and have more chicks. God reminds his people of the obvious benefits of caring for the environment.

God also shows his concern for the welfare of animals. The people are not to yoke together an ox and a donkey. Pulling a plough alongside an animal three or four times its size would be extremely painful for a donkey, and the plough may start to go round in circles (22:10)! They are also told not to muzzle an ox while it is treading the grain (25:4).

Maintaining safety in the home is equally important. In the Ancient Near East it is common for houses to be built with flat roofs. A staircase leads to the roof area, used for sleeping, relaxing or entertaining guests. If there is no protecting wall or parapet there is the danger of someone being seriously injured or even killed if they fall off the roof, so house owners are commanded to build a parapet (22:8). These simple examples demonstrate God's interest in and concern for even the small details of his people's lives.

God goes on to address the issue of vulnerable people within society. The aim of these laws is to guarantee their protection and ameliorate their situation. The first example given is that of a woman who has been divorced for reasons other than adultery (24:1–4). The intent of this law is not to promote divorce but to regulate what happens when divorce occurs (Matthew 19:7ff., 1 Corinthians 7:11ff.). The husband must give the woman a written bill of divorce, which sets her free and allows her to marry someone else. God goes on to assert the importance of newly married couples having time to spend together. The husband should not be called to serve in the army in the first year of marriage (5).

God also demands protection for families crippled by debt. Unscrupulous debt collectors, who take away millstones in lieu of money owed, will cripple a family's ability to make their daily bread. God is determined to guard the poor from commercial exploitation and from the invasion of their privacy. A man who is severely in debt needs compassion and respect.

Poor workers are often at the mercy of their employers. They have no long-term assurance of employment and are paid on a daily basis. God insists that they must be paid on time and not be deprived of their true wages (14–15). Today, recession or pandemics can cause hourly-paid workers similar problems if employment is no longer available.

Foreigners and orphans are also vulnerable and have few rights (17–21). God reminds his people of what it was like when they were foreigners and slaves in Egypt. It can be a very threatening experience to be in the minority and to have no one to take your side and defend your rights. The people of God should care for all those who are vulnerable in society just as God has cared for them. In modern times, Christians should do all they can to care for refugees from war or natural disasters.

The people of God are to be humane in the way they treat runaway slaves. Christopher Wright describes this law as astonishing: "It is diametrically opposite to the whole thrust of slave legislation in other Ancient Near Eastern law codes."[3] Runaway slaves are often punished by death, as are any who harbour them. What is prescribed

---

[3] Wright 269

168

here challenges the very institution of slavery and seems to indicate that in Israel slaves or servant workers receive far better treatment than they do in surrounding countries. The runaway slave in this case is free to choose where he will like to live: "Let them live among you wherever they like and in whatever town they choose" (23:16).

God's people are to be generous and honest in their business dealings. They are not to charge interest when they lend money to a fellow Israelite. If their neighbour is going through hard times, they must not use it as an opportunity to make money, but show their concern by lending freely to him (19–20). They are not to have two sets of weights in their house, so that they can use one set when they are buying and the other when they are selling, thereby maximising their profits (25:13–16). They must be trustworthy. They must say what they mean and keep their promises. If they make a promise to the Lord, they are to keep it (23:21; see also Jesus' teaching in Matthew 5:37).

Above all, the people of Israel are to be grateful to God. In Deuteronomy 26, Moses ends this sermon by telling the people that when they enter the land and start enjoying the rich harvest and delicious fruit, the first thing they must do is to worship the Lord. They are to give the first fruits to the Lord as a token and witness that everything they are enjoying comes from God. They are to have a great party and invite the priests and Levites to share in the party (11). The party will be for everyone, including the foreigners, widows, orphans and the poor. The whole community can rejoice together in the goodness of God. In a similar way Christians today can celebrate and give thanks for all the blessings God has given.

CHOOSE WHOM YOU WILL SERVE (27–34)

Moses is drawing to the end of his final sermon. He has pleaded with the people as passionately as he can to love God and obey his commands. He has pointed out the dangers they will encounter in the Promised Land and the blessings God wishes to give them. He concludes by calling for a response. He tells them the time has come to choose if they will serve God or not. He describes an elaborate ceremony they must perform as soon as they cross the river Jordan to demonstrate the decision they have made.

After crossing the Jordan, they are to set up some stones, cover them with plaster and write on them God's commands (27:1–4). This demonstrates the central place the word of God is always to have in their lives. Even when Moses is no longer with them, the people must constantly remember the teaching he has given them. They are then told to build an altar of unhewn stones and offer burnt offerings for sin. They will not always be able to keep God's law. They will not always be holy or obedient. The purpose of the burnt offering is to make atonement for their sin, to make them again acceptable in God's presence and to turn away his wrath. The commands remind the people they are to live under the law, and the sacrifices remind them of God's grace.

The people also have to act out a drama (9–26), which will serve as a visual demonstration of their choice. Will they obey God or not? Will they love him as he has loved them, or will they spurn his love? Once they are in the land, they must go to two mountains, which face one another across a valley near Shechem. One is Mount Ebal, the other Mount Gerizim, just two hundred metres lower. The close proximity of the two mountains, with a narrow valley in between creates a natural theatre with amazing acoustics. It is an ideal setting for a drama on a grand scale.

170

All the people are to take part. Half of them are to stand on Mount Gerizim, representing those who will obey God and who will enjoy his blessing. The other half will stand on Mount Ebal, and they will represent those who refuse to obey God, and consequently experience his judgement. As the drama proceeds, the Levites pronounce a series of twelve curses on those who disobey God, to which the people are to respond "Amen." After Moses dies, this dramatic ceremony takes place (Joshua 8:30–35).

In Deuteronomy 28, Moses proceeds to spell out the consequences of their choice. Those who seek God's favour by being faithful and obedient will be blessed in every area of their lives. Whether they live in the city or the countryside, they will be blessed in their business or on their farm. They will be blessed with many children, large flocks and herds. Their enemies will be defeated and they will be blessed wherever they go and in everything they do. But all these abundant blessings depend on their obedience (1–14).

Are these blessings for Christians? Some say yes: God does promise that if we obey and trust him, he will answer all our prayers and make us rich and prosperous and heal our diseases. A taxi driver in Singapore told me that was what he believed, but it raised the question in my mind why he was still a taxi driver, struggling to make a living. It is important we do not take these promises out of context. They are given to the people of Israel. They are promised a land. We are not. We are promised something far greater, an inheritance in God's kingdom. Paul praises God that he has blessed us in the heavenly realm with every spiritual blessing (Ephesians 1:3). Paul does not experience a life of comfort, ease and prosperity but of pain, suffering and hardship. He does not focus on material blessing, but blessings now in Jesus and in eternity.

Yet there is a spiritual principle spelled out here that does apply to us. It is inevitably true that as we walk in obedience, we will enjoy rich fellowship with Jesus and be a means of blessing to those around us. Conversely, if we do not listen to the Lord and keep going our own way we will lose out on the blessings he wants us to enjoy and share with others.

The remainder of chapter 28 makes some of the most sober reading in the whole Bible. It spells out, in stark terms, the consequence of rejecting God's grace and disobeying his commandments. The people will experience every kind of disease, disaster and tragedy. This section provides a graphic, horrific picture of what will happen to those who turn away from God (20, 22, 25, 26, 28, 30, 32). Finally, the people of Israel will experience all the plagues of Egypt. They will be enslaved again and no one will even want to buy them (68).

What is so tragic is that this is exactly what happens. The Jewish people did experience all the things prophesied here. One nation after another has persecuted the Jewish people and attempted to destroy them as a nation. The Assyrians destroyed the northern kingdom of Israel. The Babylonians destroyed Jerusalem. The Greeks put idols in the Temple. The Romans destroyed Jerusalem in 70 AD and persecuted Jews. In England Jewish people were despised, made to wear pointed hats or other marks on their clothing so people would know they were Jews. They were accused of killing God. They were barred from owning land or entering the professions. They were eventually expelled from England in 1290 by a royal decree of King Edward the first. Elsewhere they were persecuted by the Catholics during the Spanish inquisition, by Protestants following the teaching of Luther, by Orthodox Christians in Russia. Finally, six million Jews were killed in Europe in the twentieth century simply because they were Jews.

In the light of history, we need to read through this chapter again. The Jewish people were neither worse nor better than we are. They were God's chosen people and here God gives them a stark warning of the consequences of turning away from him. So, we who claim to be God's people should not imagine that he will treat us any differently if we refuse to listen to and live by his words. There is a direct correlation between spiritual blessing and our obedience. Of course, so far as the Jewish people are concerned, this is not the end of the story. They have suffered but they have also survived. Why? Because they are the people of God. God has not rejected his people, for the gift and call of God are irrevocable. Paul sees the fulfilment of that promise in the fact that so many like himself have come to faith in their Messiah. In 2017, the Jerusalem Post said there were an estimated twenty thousand Jewish Christians or Messianic Jews in Israel, and perhaps as many as three hundred and fifty thousand in the world.

The appointment of Joshua

Moses knows his time of leading the people is coming to an end. God makes it clear that Joshua is to be his successor (31:1–8, 14–23). Joshua will cross the Jordan and lead the people in the conquest of Canaan, but he has every reason to be fearful and apprehensive. Moses is a hard act to follow. He is the liberator, the nation builder, the man through whom God has wrought signs and wonders. He is the man who has spent weeks in the presence of God, whose face has shone with the glory of God. He is the man whom the Lord knows face to face. Joshua has a low opinion of himself. He is not as well qualified. He has not grown up in a palace but in a slave village. He has not been educated in a university in Egypt. He has never performed a miracle or spent days in the presence of God. But God does not want another Moses. He wants a Joshua. He wants a different kind of person with different gifts and a different temperament.

We may compare ourselves to others, to a colleague, a gifted member of the church, someone who is an able evangelist, counsellor, speaker or administrator. We may look at them and feel inadequate or incompetent. God does not want us to be somebody else. He wants us to be ourselves. He has given each of us particular gifts and a particular temperament, which he will use for his glory, providing we allow him to do so.

God is aware of how Joshua feels and gives him several promises to encourage him: "The Lord himself goes before you and will be with you; he will never leave you nor forsake you" (8). "…you will bring the Israelites into the land I promised them on oath, and I myself will be with you" (23). God gives Joshua reasons to be confident and encourages him to be "strong and courageous" (6).

The death of Moses

Before Moses dies, he writes a song to make it easier for the people to remember the truths he has been teaching them (32:1-47). Moses summarises the lessons he has been trying to teach the people. He reminds them again that in spite of all God has done, they have gone their own way and suffered the consequences. But they are God's people and he is a compassionate God. So, even though he has punished his people, he will heal them. He is the sovereign God and there is no other.

Moses then pronounces a blessing on the people, as a father would pronounce a final blessing on his family (33:1-29). He speaks of the destiny and vision God has for each tribe. Prayer is particularly requested for the tribe of Judah, and the tribe of Levi are praised for their swift action during the episode of the golden calf. An extensive blessing is given to Joseph and his two sons, Ephraim and Manasseh, which points forward to the time when they will hold a prominent place in the nation and Ephraim's name is used as a synonym for Israel (33:13–16).

Before Moses dies, God takes him to the top of one of the tallest mountains in the area, Mount Pisgah, and lets him look at the Promised Land. From the mountaintop Moses can look in every direction, north up the Jordan valley, northwest towards the region of Galilee, west towards the Mediterranean, south towards Beersheba and the Negev, and finally back to the river Jordan where the people will cross into the Promised Land. As Moses looks across the land, God reminds him of his promise: "This is the land I promised on oath to Abraham, Isaac and Jacob when I said, 'I will give it to your descendants.' I have let you see it with your eyes, but you will not cross over into it" (34:4).

Then Moses dies. He has a private funeral. He is buried (6) and even Joshua does not seem to have known the site of his grave. There is to be no shrine, no place of pilgrimage to which people can travel and worship Moses. There is to be no nostalgia, no personality cult.

The book closes with the epitaph: "Since then, no prophet has risen in Israel like Moses, whom the Lord knew face to face, who did all those signs and wonders the Lord sent him to do in Egypt—to Pharaoh and to all his officials and to his whole land. For no one has ever shown the mighty power or performed the awesome deeds that Moses did in the sight of all Israel" (34:10–12). What is remarkable about Moses is not the miracles he has done or the things he has achieved. The most important thing stated about him, and that is written first in his obituary, is that the Lord knows him face to face.

It is from that intimate relationship that everything else follows and that Moses is able to achieve all he did. He is the one who rescued Israel and founded the nation. He is the one through whom God performed amazing miracles both of judgement and of grace. He is the one through whom God spoke his words to his people, words now recorded for us which form a significant part of our Scriptures.

While other prophets minister within the covenant community, Moses is the one through whom, by God's grace, the covenant community has come into being. In that respect Moses points towards the Lord Jesus. As Moses is the mediator of the old covenant and the one through whom God has established the community of his people, so the Lord Jesus has established the new covenant through his blood and made us a people for God.

FOR PERSONAL REFLECTION

1. What actions are you taking in your church and your community to safeguard those who are vulnerable?

2. What part should Christians play in building a better world through involvement in politics, social issues, care for the environment, etc.?

3. Thank God for all the blessings we receive through Jesus. Thank him that in spite of our sinfulness we are not under a curse because Jesus has died in our place.

4. What would you like written on your epitaph? How would you like your friends and family members to remember you?